T0121667

# FOURTH MILLENNIUM

By
BLAIR YERXA

Order this book online at www.trafford.com
or email orders@trafford.com

Most Trafford titles are also available at major online book retailers.



Printed in Victoria, BC, Canada.

ISBN: 978-1-4269-0136-2 (Soft)

*We at Trafford believe that it is the responsibility of us all, as both individuals and corporations, to make choices that are environmentally and socially sound. You, in turn, are supporting this responsible conduct each time you purchase a Trafford book, or make use of our publishing services. To find out how you are helping, please visit www.trafford.com/responsiblepublishing.html*

*Our mission is to efficiently provide the world's finest, most comprehensive book publishing service, enabling every author to experience success. To find out how to publish your book, your way, and have it available worldwide, visit us online at www.trafford.com*

*Trafford rev. 01/11/2010*

**www.trafford.com**

**North America & international**
toll-free: 1 888 232 4444 (USA & Canada)
phone: 250 383 6864 • fax: 812 355 4082 • email: info@trafford.com

# CHAPTER ONE

"POTUS" HAD A LOOK of astonishment as he gazed through the glass wall at the strange objects. They were highlighted by a myriad of spotlights shining down from the metallic ceiling some fifty feet above the hangar floor. The scene, within the cavernous enclosure, seemed as if it had been transported from a Hollywood set preparing for yet another "Sci-Fi" production. It hadn't been, and the attractive and popular, recently re-elected President of the United States, was very much aware of the reality as well as the significance of this moment.

He turned to his Secretary of Defense, Michael Mullen, and said:

"I suspected something like this... There have been rumors for many years throughout the West Wing. Actually, these rumors have persisted throughout the country, even in the 'Scientific Community.' Now... finally your President is in the loop. Boy—you guys are something else. How long has this been going on Admiral? Since way back in forty-seven, I presume. I'll bet you knew about this when you were Chairman of the Joint Chiefs."

" Yes Mister President! You now know that this is a large portion of that inexplicable 'Black-Budget' that you and most past presidents have found so irritating."

The President then turned to the only other individual in the Chief Project Engineer's office, and said:

"You also Tim? You knew about this before I did?"

Tim Crawford, Special Agent in Charge of the Presidential Protective Division of the Secret Service, looked a little flustered, then answered:

"Yes Sir, but only a short time before you. I came out with our regular 'Advance-Team' a couple of weeks ago. It didn't involve much probing because everyone at this facility is Top Secret, Special-Access, cleared."

The three individuals again took in the scene beyond the glass wall. There were only the five Air Force personnel dressed in their flight suits, and the Chief Project Engineer standing between the two strange craft. The other technicians and engineers remained off of the hangar floor, viewing the proceedings from the other glass walled offices and shops that encircled the vast chamber.

It was time for the maiden flight of their super secret Anti-Grav One, normally referred to as "AG-1", and it was about to lift off from its underground location without fanfare, or any publicity whatever. It was a true stealth operation.

The long sought anti-gravity drive system had finally been achieved in this Nevada desert's proving ground. It had taken decades to engineer and then achieve a space ship utilizing this long sought after propulsion system, and a ship that was suitable for human occupation. Reverse engineering of the long ago acquired UFO known as Aztec-One, had been delayed until the development of our own advanced digital computer technology had finally made it possible to solve this complicated and puzzling ship. It had been found well out in the cactus speckled fields south of Aztec, New Mexico in 1947. Obviously, our engineers and scientists had to wait for our own advances in the then mysterious disciplines of: Composites, Metallurgy, Chemistry, Quantum-physics and Astronomy. All these accomplishments were necessary before we could produce this extraordinary ship on a human sized scale. It was only very recently that enough "Anti-matter" fuel had been produced at the circular four mile long Fermi Lab's *collider* to propel the new ship on its upcoming brief, lightning fast, mission.

It had been sixty-six years since the partially damaged space ship had been recovered from the New Mexico desert just three hundred miles northwest of the much publicized Roswell site. The scattered remains of the ship found at the Roswell site had also been utilized in the reverse engineering program. Some of this recovered equipment made it possible to dissect sophisticated parts of Aztec-One without removing such identical parts from that nearly intact UFO. During most of those intervening years the mysterious disc shaped craft was painstakingly studied and now sat stoically on its man-made pedestal. This was located inside the large underground hangar located approximately 120 miles northwest of Nellis Air Force Base and well beyond the nightly glow of the bright lights of Las Vegas, Nevada.

When he was transported to this site from the Nellis Airfield aboard "Marine One," the President had expected his helicopter to land at the Groom Lake facility in Area 51. Instead they landed just south of Cactus Peak at a well camouflaged facility. They were still on the huge Nellis Test Range but they weren't at the legendary, and no longer very secret, Groom Lake Base. Furthermore, the President had been briefed that the infamous "Area 51" facility had been shut down and dismantled back in the late Nineteen Nineties. He still believed that they might be heading in that direction when they left the Nellis airstrip. Like many other "well informed" Americans, the President believed that there still were some top-secret operations going on beneath the dry sandy soils of Groom Lake. Now he realized that he was correct, except these operations weren't at that Groom Lake base; they now existed at a base carved into the side of a mountain some seventy miles to the northwest of the old facility.

"Prickly Peak" as the base was known by its small group of scientists and technicians, was a truly well kept secret, rivaling the "Manhattan Project" which had been concerned with nuclear fission and the development of the atom bomb during the Second World War. This small group of dedicated individuals involved with the anti-gravity space vehicle development, maintained families and homes in nearby Tonopah, Nevada. They all had effective cover-stories concerning where they worked and what they did for a living. These *stories* proved to be very difficult for an outsider to refute, and to this point they had been quite successful with their little charades. The secrecy surrounding the nations 'Anti-Grav' operation remained tight and the base remained secure.

Now, having descended some seventy feet into the desert floor and then two-hundred feet north beneath Cactus Mountain, the President and his two companions continued to study the bizarre scene before them.

Next to the twenty-two foot diameter *non-existent* alien space craft, loomed the much larger human sized ship. It had been painstakingly fabricated over the past fifteen years as the different systems found aboard the Aztec ship and the Roswell wreckage were exposed and their mysteries solved. The new ship looked like a close copy of the Aztec ship, only the dimensions had grown to accommodate its new human passengers. With ground struts retracted, the big new space-ship hovered nine feet above the concrete floor of the hangar while the only sound coming from its interior was a soft electrical purr. The ship was fifty-seven feet in diameter and slightly over fourteen feet thick at its center. The outer edge was no more than four feet thick and projected a faint, rather eerie, orange glow.

Hal Proch pressed a button on his palm sized activator, then handed the device to Air Force Major Tom Brice, the recently designated aircraft commander.

"Its all yours Major," Hal Proch stated with a broad smile.

At that moment, the center elevator slid silently down to within a few inches of the hangar floor. Joining Major Brice as he moved towards the elevator were, Captain Janet Hulse, along with Master Sergeant Robert Carmody, and Technical Sergeants Lilly French and Norman Johnson. Only two persons could fit inside the little elevator at a time, so Major Brice sent the other crew members up, then followed alone. Just before the elevator rose for the final time, he saluted Hal Proch and the numerous other technicians that had now gathered by the shop entrances some distance back. As the transparent enclosure ascended, Major Brice turned towards the President and gave him a sharp military salute. The President returned the gesture, followed by a less formal thumbs up sign, and a broad smile.

At precisely 0100 hours local, 0700 hours 'Zulu,' on April 16$^{th}$ 2013, the great disc moved silently out into the enormous adjacent underground shaft. The surface doors above the 70 foot deep shaft, slid open and AG-1 lifted stealthily into the cool night sky.

* * *

The all Air Force crew had repeated these maneuvers hundreds of times at their consoles in their elaborate AG-1 simulator. They also had been aboard the actual star-ship on numerous occasions. They could often be found sitting at the consoles while familiarizing themselves with the feel and ambiance of the magical ship as they powered up the drive and anti-gravity mechanisms. This, however, was the first time that they would actually take the ship beyond its protective hangar and out into the chilly atmosphere, and then on up into frigid lifeless space.

Everything went as programmed and they shot straight up into the moonless, star filled firmament above the desert. There wasn't the slightest sensation of motion; no "G-force" pressure. Their new center-of-gravity had now become a twenty foot diameter composite disc located at the base of the ship. Beneath this innocuous disc lurked innumerable "black-boxes" that performed the gravitational miracle. The crew had not been required to wear "G-suits," therefore, they were all dressed in comfortable Air Force Nomax flight suits. They each had there international orange lined nylon flight jackets, and all had previously brought aboard their personal "fly-away" bags. These were stored beneath their individual bunks which had been neatly tailored into the circular interior of the ship and hidden by thick, light-proof and nearly sound proof, draw curtains. These crew-member satchels contained changes of clothing, toiletries and whatever else each deemed necessary for a trip of approximately one week. The food lockers were loaded with enough rations for two weeks and the medical locker was fully equipped and loaded.

Major Brice was a Command Pilot and had been trained as a test pilot at Edwards Air Force Base located in the raw Mojave desert. Captain Hulse wore senior navigator wings and had been studying the intricate disciplines of space and interstellar navigation for the past two years. The three non-commissioned officers were qualified air crew members. Although none of the "Five," as yet, were rated astronauts; all five had been through the infamous pressure chamber at Castle Air Force Base in the San Joaquin Valley. There, they had experienced rapid decompression at a simulated forty-three thousand feet of altitude. From there, they all proceeded to Texas where they completed their astronaut training.

Their final training program had dealt with space-medicine and the practical application of the unique first-aide techniques that might be necessary during their mission. This last ten day program they attended as a team and during this they were informed that there would not be a medical officer among the crew. They were told that the planners had decided that they all must be aware of the medical problems that might arise during their exceptional mission and how to treat them. The planners had decided that a designated medical officer might become the one incapacitated and that such and addition would require eliminating another more critical position. They were also informed that they were moving into a place that might bring on unknown medical problems. Each member was well aware of this possibility and accepted the challenge with courage.

The training had included practicing first-aide techniques on small lifelike fiberglass dummies. When, during this training, it became time to perform mouth-to-mouth resuscitation on these uninviting training aides, Tom Brice turned to face Janet Hulse. He focused his vision rather intently on her alluring lips and remarked in his best "Treasure of Sierra Madre" imitation:

"Dummies… We don't need no stinking dummies!"

This had resulted in immediate laughter from his subordinate sergeants, while Janet merely shook her head slowly and smiled provocatively at her newly appointed commanding officer

* * * .

Now, they all were soaring effortlessly above the quiet Nevada desert with ever increasing speed.

"Thirty thousand meters Boss," Navigator Janet Hulse informed Major Brice.

Brice touched his display and the star-ship made an abrupt turn to the north. Again, there was no sensation of movement within AG-1. Small bright numerals on all the panels indicated a forward speed of Mach 6.2 as measured against a stationary fixed point on earth.

Aircraft Commander Brice turned to Captain Hulse and said:

"Hey Jan—ain't this grand. We're flying over four thousand miles an hour and we just made a ninety-degree turn. Wow! No vertigo—no nausea! Anti-grav is great!"

Beautiful dark haired Janet Hulse quickly replied:

"It's what we all have been working for Boss. Now tell me, why did we spend so much time in that dreadful centrifuge…?"

The three other crew members turned their well padded swivel chairs away from their colorful panel displays and smiled at the two officers. Sergeant Carmody then chimed in:

"The guys back at Vandenberg won't believe me when I tell them about this. Look at this Jan; these gravity settings must be accurate."

With this the sergeant dropped his pen to the floor and it fell as if he was still sitting at his desk back in his office at the enormous Central California Coast Air Force Base, affectionately known by its personnel as "Vandy-land."

Sergeant Carmody's unmilitary and familiar response to the captain was fairly normal behavior for "close-knit" aircrew members when alone in their aircraft. Military protocol often remained on-hold while away from public scrutiny. This sort of thing had been going on as long as air crews existed. Normally, nick-names were used and the Aircraft Commander was simply referred to as "Boss."

On this mission they were: "Boss" and "Jan," while Carmody was called "Rob." Red haired Technical Sergeant Lilly French was naturally referred to as "Red," and jovial Technical Sergeant Norman Johnson was simply called "Norm." Boss, Jan, Rob, Red and Norm, were the five individuals charged with testing the most expensive aircraft ever constructed. Each was aware of the enormous responsibility and all were confident that they were up to the task.

Jan began to punch in the solar coordinates that were critical to the test flight plan for the new ship. They were required to fly a polar orbit circumnavigation of the earth at increasing altitudes and increasing speeds. They would continue this process until their altitude was far above the orbital track of the moon. This is when they would "open-it-up." They were to use the "Impulse Projection Warp Drive" system out near its full power limits. No one knew what these limits were, hence this crucial test. The amount of the new "anti-matter" fuel necessary for this mission was so tiny that it was often referred to as microscopic.

"Altitude one-hundred and twenty kilometers Boss, speed mach thirty-six," Jan reported in a flat response to the readings. "Can you believe how quickly we reached forty thousand 'clicks' per hour, and also how well our Repulse Radar worked in avoiding space junk."

On completion of the fourth orbit their speed had reached Mach 100 and it now took little more than an hour to complete the next orbit of their cloud spun blue and white home planet. It wasn't long before their ever increasing distance from earth had passed 100,000 miles. Their smooth acceleration, with its ever expanding orbital plane, continued for three more hours. At this point they were well beyond the moon's orbit and over one half a million miles above the earth on an orbital track that was 90° opposed to the solar system's sidereal-plane. Their speed was no longer calibrated against the speed of sound, instead, the percentages came up against light-speed or "warp-speed." They had just passed 1% "warp" or nearly 1,900 miles per second. This is approximately the time when they lost all electronic communication with their home base. They were all aware that such a phenomenon would probably occur, but none of them knew when such a moment of total isolation would take place.

"Jesus Christ! We're out of touch with the world and were now going seven million miles an hour. Even on this three million mile orbit it will take less than twenty-eight minutes to accomplish the next revolution of earth!"

Rob offered this bit of information to a growing disbelief that now permeated the flight deck of AG-1. They also had been made aware of the possibility of these speeds and distances in training, but the actual event was still more than a little disturbing.

Boss swiveled his chair around to face the others and said:

"You all realize from our training, that we are now entering a different time continuum than our friends back home, hence the term warp or 'Time-Warp.' This, however, is not the 'Warp Speed' of 'Star Trek,' which was a thousand times light speed. We'll let the science fiction writers deal with those speeds. Time is passing more slowly here than back on earth, and this is why we have just lost all communications with our home base. This science is just being formulated and we are to be a big part of that formulation. The tests with our astronauts on the space shuttle missions indicated that Einstein, of course, was correct in his "Special and General theories of Relativity," when it came to the slowing of time as an object approached the speed of light. This is the slowing of time in relationship to earth time. Time to us is still the same and our aging process remains the same. All previous experiments testing this theory were made at infinitely slower speeds than we are expected to accomplish, and their time changes were measured in milliseconds. We have no formula for the relative rate of time change. That is why this crew has been picked. None of us are married and our individual responsibilities to others on earth, are minimal. This is hardly a ringing endorsement concerning our personal humanity."

Sergeant Johnson responded to this with a sad expression:

"Are we really that cold Boss?"

"Not at all Norm, I was just being foolish. In fact, you are the most pleasant and friendly group that I have ever worked with. It is just a fact concerning our selection."

Norm looked relieved at this remark as did the other crew members.

Major Brice continued with his informal briefing as the ship sped on its lightning fast orbit of Planet Earth.

"The feeling at headquarters is that we will probably return a few weeks beyond the time we spend in space on our computer and on this ships internal clocks. This, of course, depends upon how fast we can get this 'saucer' to move. I was told by Hal Proch that we should be prepared for the possibility of a few months change in time, or maybe even a year or two. Just think of the back pay we'll receive if this is the case."

With this remark the crew members responded, in near unison: "Right On!"

Major Brice now began the final ascent to the previously established distance from the earth, out to ( 0.20 a.u.), or a radius of approximately 18 million miles with an orbital circumference around the earth of close to 120 million miles. This maneuver took a few more hours due to numerous incremental calibration checks, during which time Lilly French and Norman Johnson used the ships galley to cook up some fine meals. Although they actually were previously prepared frozen dinners, they proved to be excellent. Lilly put on some soft classical music and dimmed the lights in the control room. They all sat down at the central table while the ships trusty computers searched for their proper final orbit.

The circular main cabin of their ship had a vaulted ceiling which extended out just beyond their individual consoles. The high point of this ceiling was directly over the center of their round dining table. The five tall chairs which they now occupied, were not attached to the hard surfaced deck as were the padded chairs at their work stations. This wasn't necessary in a ship that enjoyed its own center of gravity.

A sweeping span of soft pastel colored imbedded lights shone down from the domed ceiling and helped establish a warm and pleasant ambiance for the ships interior. It was no longer necessary, nor desired, to have the interior of their craft spartanly finished in cold metallic surfaces and equipped with lifeless gray nylon safety belts with stainless steel buckles. Safety belts were no longer required nor desired. The interior wall of their ship was painted with varying shades of attractive colors, and although muted, they proved to have the desired psychological affect envisioned by the designers when involved with the final assembly of AG-1. Every practical convenience was consider when preparing for the five crew members comfort, as all those involved in the fabrication of this ship were well aware of the dangers that faced these brave young people.

After reaching their designated orbital position, the Aircraft Commander punched in the codes to increase the spaceships speed to the limits that had been established by the engineers. Obtaining this enormous increase in speed would consume an additional ten hours. With the codes entered, each member of the crew took turns using the limited shower and toilet facilities, then all except Sergeant Carmody pulled aside the heavy curtains that shielded their individual bunks. All of their private sleeping accommodations were located along the outer periphery of the control room. Carmody would stand the first two hour watch, even though there was little that he could do prior to acquiring their previously established maximum speed. Their increase in speed was also accomplished incrementally so that the specialized instrumentation packages could be accurately re-calibrated. Major Brice was aware that they could probably go to their pre-designated maximum speed instantly, without any physiological or structural damage, but that the calibrations were essential for future scientific study.

* * *

The crew members awakened surprisingly refreshed after spending their first sleep period in space. Less than an hour following their initial seven hour sleep, a persistent bell sounded and the red and green lights on their control panels indicated that they had finally reached 90% of the speed of light. The understanding was that they would not make any attempt to pierce the "Light-Speed Barrier," on this initial flight, therefore Major Brice had programmed the drive computer to stop accelerating at 90% indicated. The scientists back at base were pretty well convinced that light-speed was a true barrier, unlike the speed of sound. These learned scientists had unanimously determined that traveling at 90% of the speed of light was pushing the envelope of survivability far enough. This was certainly the prevailing thought in each of their gifted minds, especially prior to establishing a working formula for what they referred to as a *Dimensional-Time-Jump.*

Lilly checked the scope that she had trained on their now much smaller pale blue home planet.

"It's become a blur!" she exclaimed. "The surface of Earth has become a blur!"

Instantly the entire crew looked out of the front view ports and the background stars had also blurred into curved streaks as their craft continued on in its huge orbit around their home planet.

"That proves that we have moved into a much different time continuum," remarked Major Brice. "We have also become invisible to all earth-bound visual searches, as well as electronic instrumentation. Now the question is, just how far forward are we projecting ourselves?"

With this provocative hypothetical question, the entire crew stared openly from one to the other. Then, as if by some silent signal, they all began to smile. Each member of the crew now realized the enormity of their adventure as they hurtled on through cold space. To a person, they felt a certain pride at being hand picked for this mission. There weren't any fear induced pangs of regret among these young pioneers. Rob Carmody secretly hoped that their *time-jump* would be a big one. He felt that he had endured enough pain and sorrow during the recent decade. He believed that he would welcome a jump into another decade, *even* another century.

Tom Brice looked once more out of the forward view screen and felt a wave of relief wash over his entire body. Although the stars in his vision were streaked, attesting to their enormous speed, they were still there. He hadn't discussed with his faithful crew one other little detail of Albert Einstein's theories concerning relativity. Hal Proch had brought it up, almost casually prior to their departure. It seems that Albert Einstein had also considered the possibility that an encapsulated moving object approaching the speed of light, might expand in size. That is, as Chief Project Engineer Proch explained, while dramatically flinging his hands wide apart:

"Such an expansion might be *infinite.*"

"Thank God for the '*might*' in Einstein's explanation," murmured Tom Brice as he now realized that such a catastrophic event had not occurred.

# CHAPTER TWO

MAJOR THOMAS BRICE WAS born at Fitzsimmons Army Hospital in Aurora, Colorado in 1980. His father, Master Sergeant Phillip Brice, had been stationed at Lowry Air Force Base at that time. Following Phillip's retirement from the Air Force, the Brice family remained in their quiet off-base suburb located just a few miles east of the booming city of Denver.

The whole Colorado experience provided many happy memories for young Tom. He grew up in what could be described as a rather comfortable life style when compared with most. His father became a successful Real Estate Broker following his military retirement. He was able to provide his wife and young Tom with a fine home, as well as entertaining and informative travels throughout the western states. Phillip was a sportsman and this love he passed onto Tom. Tom played team sports in school including baseball and football. He felt that he was a little too short for basketball. He also developed some ability in individual sports, such as tennis and golf. In the winter, Phillip would often take the family up to the alpine ski-runs just west of Denver. Tom especially liked the downhill runs at Berthoud Pass, upon which he became an accomplished skier.

His father's wish was that young Thomas would eventually enter the Air Force Academy located 55 miles south on route I-25, just north of Colorado Springs. The family was elated when, in fact, Thomas did qualify for that prestigious military academy. He graduated near the top of his class in 2001, and then went directly into pilot training.

For many years there had been an unwritten practice in pilot training to steer the cadets who were under 5 feet 10 inches tall, towards fighter-pilot training. Many years earlier, at the start of World War Two, the primary fighter plane in the then Army Air Corps was the P-40 "Warhawk," with its limited cockpit space. By the time the larger fighter planes arrived with their bubble canopy's, the Air Corps commanders had decided that the shorter pilots were better equipped for aerial combat in all fighter aircraft. It had something to do with hand-eye coordination and reaction time. Therefore, the practice of using a cadets height as a factor in advanced pilot training continued. There have been a few outstanding exceptions to this rule, but it still continued as an unwritten guideline.

Thomas Brice was a very well coordinated five foot nine inch candidate. He became an exceptional pilot and later an instructor pilot, which led to his selection as a Test Pilot at Edwards Air Force Base, in California. From here it was on to astronaut training in Texas and eventually this assignment. With the limited space in their "saucer," the height limitation for crew members had been established at five nine. The limits were said to be based on the size of the crews bunks; they were barely six feet long and the planners were well aware of the fact that humans needed three inches more than their height for a bed or bunk to be comfortable. There were, in fact, other more compelling reasons for the height requirements, such as the size of the ships access hatch and the elevator.

Tom Brice had a pleasant, friendly nature in dealing with others. However, when it came time for him to become a military professional and give orders, he was articulate and decisive. There was never a question concerning what he was demanding, and he wouldn't tolerate less than excellence. The crew fully understood the two sides of their "Boss's" behavior and they knew when he was kidding and when he was serious, by the changes in resonance of his deep voice. The Major had natural command presence in expression and appearance, and the crew appreciated these characteristics in their leader. He had a full head of brown curly hair which framed his broad face and strong jaw. Tom Brice exuded leadership in all areas of his behavior, and he was identified as a natural future candidate for senior command by his superiors.

*    *    *

Anti-Grav One's mission plan called for maintaining their wide orbit at 90% of the speed of light for 96 hours. Following this, it was estimated that it would take about 13 hours to return to their "Prickly Peak" base in the Nevada desert. In total, the length of their mission was estimated to require approximately 136 hours of encapsulated time. The AG-1 Commander was to have some latitude with these time frames, as there were a number of scientific experiments that the crew were required to accomplish. However, one of the primary reasons that this was a manned space flight was to test the *time-warping* or *time-dilation* effects on the human body. Major Brice was well aware that they were being used as "Guinea Pigs" in this experiment. A fact that he kept to himself, although the entire crew was also fully aware of this as well.

Meanwhile, Chief Project Engineer Proch planned to keep a small team of personnel permanently manning the tiny communications center at their home-base. Although, he did not pass this on to the crew, he planned a 10 year manning program to "stand-by" on their coded frequencies, for communications contact reestablishment with AG-1. He had a premonition that their mission might last a number of years. He had told Major Brice that it might last a year or even two in earth time. However, he had a strong suspicion that it might be much longer before he would welcome home his little band of space travelers. Deep space travel would require extreme speeds and they had to come up with a definitive rule to make projections on how far subsequent space travelers would be able to soar out into the future.

Hal Proch was, through private briefings with some senior project scientists, aware that this historic mission might just propel his five volunteers into a totally different era. He and the scientists also considered the possibility that AG-1 might just make a jump into another dimension. The eleven dimensions of the "String-Theory" had been openly discussed among these scientists, during the past few years. This was now referred to as the "M" Theory. Most members of the Scientific Community were now convinced that there probably were dimensions beyond our recognizable boundaries of space and time. They had impressed upon the volunteers that the mission was quite dangerous, however they did not go into these mysterious properties of Quantum Mechanics. Hal decided not to venture too far into the unknown when briefing the five brave souls just prior to their departure.

*How can I?* he considered. *I can't be specific about situations that none of us are certain of. That's the reason for this mission—to answer these damned questions.*

These, and similar thoughts filled Hal's mind following the departure of AG-1. He was searching for emotional relief, even vindication to cover his rising guilt in not being a little more specific about the dangers that faced the intrepid crew.

*Christ! I would have gone myself. I did volunteer—too old they said. Too damned old…*

Hal's thoughts continued on this idea in his vain attempt to relieve himself of a steadily growing concern.

* * *

Master Sergeant Robert Carmody was born to a working class family in Bridgeport, Connecticut, in 1977. His younger sister Jane was now a successful software editor in Boston and Rob stayed in close communication with her, his only sibling. He had joined the Air Force immediately upon his completion of high school in the spring of 1995. Carmody was the oldest member of the crew and had experienced "close-in" combat on the troubled streets of Baghdad. However, most of his military career had been spent at Vandenberg Air Force Base. He was an aircraft and missile maintenance specialist and was the designated Crew Chief for this mission.

Not long after his marriage in 2006, Sergeant Carmody lost his attractive wife Joan in a tragic automobile accident. The small car she was driving was broad-sided by a large SUV while shopping in the nearby city of Santa Maria. The other driver was concentrating on her cell-phone when she ran a traffic light at the McCoy and Miller Street intersection. Sergeant Carmody never remarried following this and although he passed the recent rather meticulous psychological evaluation, a dark void remained deep in his soul. He had since covered his sorrow with work and night school classes. During the intervening years he was able to acquire an Associate Degree from Allan Hancock Community College in Santa Maria, and later a BA Degree in Business

Management from The University of La Verne. That fine school had a very convenient extension branch at Vandenberg and Carmody, along with many others, took full advantage of this opportunity.

Although he had been through a great deal of emotional suffering in his personal life, the sergeant maintained a positive outlook and enjoyed a dry sense of humor. Carmody was well liked by his crew members and was often the center of attention during their informal get-togethers. Rob Carmody was a stocky five foot eight inch tall son of a third generation Irish immigrant father and a mother whose Dutch ancestry dated back to the settlers of New Amsterdam. He had that easy to sunburn reddish skin, blue eyes and light brown hair, physical characteristics that were passed down through the centuries from his Irish and Dutch ancestors. Sergeant Carmody's full head of hair was beginning to become flecked with gray, a testament to the difficulties of his more recent past.

Carmody was often told by his crew members that he was full of "Blarney," yet he would simply wink away such well intentioned comments with some self depreciating witticism. Master Sergeant Carmody was a maintenance expert and had spent months learning how to repair the complicated mechanical and electronic equipment on AG-1. During much of his military career he had worked on missiles deep in the "Silos" at Vandenberg, yet, some of this new electronic equipment was so sophisticated that the project engineers merely instructed Carmody on how to change the "black-boxes." He was supplied with a large inventory of these replacement parts. The sergeant had a natural feel for engineering and could sense when a part was going to need repair, or replacement. This he found a little more difficult to do when dealing with micro chips hidden in their inscrutable black plastic containers. Rob was an old fashioned, *hands-on*, type of guy, in his work with machinery and in his dealings with his far more sensitive human companions as well.

*    *    *

On board AG-1, with the computers handling much of the operation, all the crew members had time to reflect about the immediate past that may have led to this operation.

During the decade directly preceding the departure of AG-1, the five crew members, along with everyone else world-wide, had endured the steadily growing negative affects of "Global Warming."

First, in the years stretching from 2003 through 2006, there were the political denials that such a thing actually existed. It was consider by many as an attempt by a few to embarrass those in power. The Kyoto Protocols had passed by without the ratification of the United States Congress. It was felt by the U.S. Administration that submitting to the rather harsh Kyoto guidelines would be extremely detrimental to our national economy. It was determined by many scientists that these accords wouldn't accomplished anything positive. They were based on flawed science and written in a way to punish the most powerful nations.

Members of the U.S. Administration, both in the White House and in Congress were quite correct about this. However, not making a more concerted effort to clean up the damage being done by the burning of fossil fuels, and curtailing the future use of such fuels, was unquestionably causing serious problems.

In December 2004, the great Indonesian earthquake and resulting *Tsunami* should have alerted the majority of people concerned, to the catastrophic affect of natural disasters. One quarter of a million individuals died in that one. The numbers killed were now growing well beyond those of previous events, so was the physical damage. Tying this disaster to global warming was a *reach* that many did not accept. However, the 2005 hurricane season, crowned by Katrina and Rita should have been the definitive alarm.

Still, the nay-sayers persisted and America continued to purchase gas guzzling vehicles. By early 2008, the high price of gas finally began to take its inevitable toll on these vehicles. With steadily increasing problems in the Middle-East and soaring gas prices, smaller, more efficient cars, once again gained their earlier market-share.

The documentary films concerned with the shrinking ice caps now pervaded the media outlets. They graphically illustrated the melting of *above sea level* ice. They also dramatically displayed the actual disappearance of northern latitude glaciers. No longer could the charge of *point on point* slanted coverage be leveled. By early 2010, a large majority of the worlds population was aware that global warming was with us and that it was severe. Record hot summers throughout the heavily populated Northern Hemisphere from 2009 on, had fueled the most destructive run of foul weather in recorded history. Even the severe winter weather of 2008/9 along the northern tier of states failed to sway the scientists from their beliefs concerning the warming of planet earth. Record breaking freezes in certain areas were part of the destabilization of the earth's weather they rightfully explained to their very vocal skeptics.

All attempts to rebuild Katrina ravaged New Orleans and the Southern Mississippi coastline were met with increasingly savage storm seasons. Finally, that great city remained habitable for only a dramatically reduced population. The large New Orleans oil port continued operations, although by 2013 the production from the drilling platforms in the Gulf had been seriously reduced. By that time, many of these Gulf of Mexico drilling rigs had either been abandoned or destroyed. The effect of these events on gasoline prices had finally forced the public acceptance of tiny hybrid cars and had, also, sped up the development and use of hydrogen fuel cell powered automobile engines. By the time the astronauts climbed aboard AG-1, nearly half of the motor vehicles, including large trucks, had switched to clean burning hydrogen. There were still problems with distribution of this fuel source and the engineers were still working on increasing distribution facilities in order to lower the costs of operation.

The ultimate question at this moment was: "Are we too late?"

Major Tom Brice posed this question to his crew as they openly discussed these national and international situations.

"God knows!" remarked Rob Carmody. "I really mean that. Only God knows! If we really are being projected forward a few months or even years of earth time—only he knows what we will find when we return. Will those damned storms still be increasing in their ferocity? What about the ice-caps? What the hell will happen if a large portion of that above-sea-level ice at the South Pole keeps melting?"

"I don't think I'd invest in a villa by the sea right now," interrupted Norm Johnson.

This remark elicited nods of agreement around the circular interior of their remarkable space craft.

Now it was time for speculation.

"What if a great deal of time really has passed?," remarked Janet. "I mean years! What if those who meet us don't know anything about our mission? What if the United States no longer exists and the terrorists have taken over!?

"Easy Captain. Take it easy Jan. We could all go on speculating like this endlessly. We must have faith that the *jump* will be no more than a few months, or a year or two at most, and that things will not have changed that much."

Tom Brice said this with a reassuring tone, yet some of Janet Hulse's questions left an air of apprehension in his mind as well as in the thoughts of the rest of the crew. They all knew that they were blazing their way into an anxious unknown.

Tom looked reassuringly at his emotionally troubled friend, walked over to her chair and placed his arm over her shoulder.

"I'm with you throughout this thing Janet… I'll always be with you, whenever you need me."

Janet Hulse felt comforted by Tom Brice's reaction to her emotional stress concerning the questionable immediate future of her beloved nation. She had a great deal of respect for her aircraft commander. It was respect that had been earned by Tom over the recent months of training that they had shared. She also was well aware that there was a little bit more than comforting in his softly spoken remarks and subtle hug.

The close-quarters of their ship brought everyone into shared familiarity. Prior to lift-off, each one of the crew thought that some emotional problems and even some hostility might develop during the voyage. All of the crew members of AG-1 were pleasantly surprised at the overall compatibility of the group as they entered their third day together.

*These certainly are confined spaces for individuals used to having their own space*, thought Lilly, almost verbalizing her thoughts.

Along with this, she and the other two sergeants had become aware of Boss Tom's growing affection for Janet Hulse. It was quite obvious to all of them, and although amusing to the sergeants, the situation seemed to have no detrimental affect on their genuine feelings of friendship towards one another, including the two officers. During those months of training together, they had developed real friendships. However, during that time the sergeants had continued to address their officers formally, in accordance with military protocol. Now, even that formality was gone and all the crew were developing true affection towards one another.

The crew of AG-1 now looked forward to a pleasant trip, and due to the limited work schedule, each found time to joke and clown around for the benefit of all. They all seemed to possess well develop senses of humor which added to their enjoyment of the otherwise, extremely dangerous trip.

# CHAPTER THREE

AG-1 CONTINUED ON IN its smooth orbital track and the bright star-streaks remained splayed across the large forward view screen. There were other view screens aboard the space ship. These were the flat 19 inch computer screens at each console. AG-1 also had a large flat 60 inch high-definition television screen located on the opposite side of the crew compartment. The crew members, along with their favorite music, also brought their favorite movies which they would play after rather comical votes on which DVD would be next.

"God! Not that turkey," or "You didn't really bring that one—did you?"

On the third evening out they played the three hour long wartime drama "Destination Stalingrad." This Second World War love story, which took place in war ravaged Russia, was well received by the crew. Jan said, "I see why it was nominated for an Academy Award, however, Sonya's love affair with her 'Mishka' was never fully resolved. That really pissed me off!"

"Now, now Jan—it was only a movie. Now—if it was an affair between you and I, I'll promise you, it would have been resolved."

Tom Brice said this with an evil grin, however, there was more than a little sparkle in his steady blue eyes. Once again Janet was reminded about how Tom felt about her, and she reacted to this remark with a pert and rather quick grimace, then stuck out her tongue. The rest of the crew reacted with groans and a couple of friendly cat calls.

* * *

Born and raised in Santa Monica, California, Captain Janet Hulse graduated from nearby UCLA in 2006 with a BS Degree in Physics. She was in the AFROTC program there and received the gold bars of an Air Force Second Lieutenant upon graduation. She went on to flight school in Texas, following graduation. She received her navigator wings in 2007 and followed that with advanced training in Celestial Navigation and Astro-Physics. Early in 2008 she was promoted to the rank of First Lieutenant. After being cleared for Top Secret Special Access, she entered the AG-1 Program and in 2011 she went through the same astronaut training school that Major Brice and the others attended. On completion of this training she received the silver tracks of a Captain.

Janet stood 5'3" tall, and although she weighed only 110 pounds, she was quite athletic and surprisingly strong. She had a graceful and powerful athleticism that defied her diminutive size. Dark haired, brown eyed Janet Hulse was an extremely beautiful young woman. Her fellow officers as well as the many enlisted men that came within her aura, during her brief Air Force career, found it difficult to deal with her on a professional level. When trying to discuss some important technical detail with her, they found her remarkable face and form very distracting. Janet's hair was cut fairly short in order to comply with crew-member regulations, yet its soft natural waves framed the flawless skin of her iridescent face. Her natural loveliness caused these distractions from the young men and a touch of classic envy from the young women that were in her company.

When Janet was out in their ships tiny galley, Sergeant Carmody cryptically informed everyone:

"She has the power!"

There are beautiful women that sometimes have little idea just how much "power" they have over men. Most, by the time they reach Janet's 28 years, have come to realize this power. Janet was no exception, and she wasn't so sure that it was a blessing. The self-conscious behavior of young men in her presence she used to find flattering, but now it was simply irritating. Older men, such as Major Brice, didn't display this awkwardness. However, he did, through many subtle signs, indicate how he felt about her. His latest remark only intensified her belief that he was more than casually interested. She now realized that she too was attracted to his handsome face, pleasant manner, and intelligence.

Captain Janet Hulse, much like her boss, had natural leadership ability. This was rather rare in young women, yet, many came out of officer training with a new perspective on their own personal values and abilities. She learned how to project from her soft delicate appearance a hard decisiveness, through look and manner; which would bring her skeptical young subordinates back to reality. Janet was an effective officer and a welcome member of the entire crew.

Janet had tolerated a few boy-friends over the years, however, she found most of the young men that she happened to meet, intellectually inferior. She knew that some of them were bright, but their awkward behavior became a rather unpleasant turn-off. She had finally come to the realization that if she was ever going to have a family, it would be with an older, more mature man.

* * *

The crewmembers now sat around the center table; the plastic trays which held their frozen dinners had been cleared and placed in the compactor. The playing cards were out and the poker chips were divided up. It was now their fourth evening together in these cramped quarters, and they all found it rather remarkable how increasingly well they got along with each other.

Sergeant Norman Johnson proved to be the best poker player and for the third night in a row he quickly became the chip leader.

"I guess we know what your AFSC should be Norm," said Rob Carmody:

"Gambler Superintendent. That would be nine-level."

"Yea—Yea!" Norm's matter of fact response amused the crew.

"I have been in a few poker games in my day. That's the nature of security—they either need you immediately with full concentration and physical effort, or you just sit around and wait. It's something like combat: Long stretches of boredom, punctuated by brief moments of terror."

* * *

Technical Sergeant Norman Johnson knew quite a lot about combat having completed three tours of duty as a Security Policeman in Baghdad, Iraq from 2005 through 2007. Norm had been wounded by an IED during his final tour, however, the shrapnel wounds had not been career threatening. He had taken hits in his left leg and arm. All the shrapnel had been removed without any serious weakening of his formidable athletic ability. Norm was a fine swimmer, golfer and tennis player as well as a good poker player. Although these skills were hardly related, he loved the competition they all provided.

Norm was born in 1983 and raised in Washington, D.C. His father was African American and his mother was Asian. He liked to compare himself to Tiger Woods who enjoyed a similar genealogy. He readily admitted, when it came to golf, that he was no Tiger…

"My golf game needs work—terrible short-game."

He was, however, a fine athlete and a very pleasant young man. He had joined the Air Force on completion of high school in 2001. He was trained as a Security Policeman and was now the Security Chief among the tiny crew. He hadn't been convinced that such a position was needed until the mission directors explained that because of the possible *time-jump*, they might find themselves in an unknown, or even a hostile environment, upon their return to earth.

Norm Johnson had attended "on-base" University of Maryland extension courses in Business, while stationed at Andrews Air Force Base near Washington, D.C. He also attended some on-campus classes as well, with the large university being only a few miles from his home. In 2010, Norm received his Batchelor of Arts Degree in Business Administration from Maryland with his proud family in attendance. Norm believed that adding this accomplishment to his résumé may have been a deciding factor in his being picked for this special mission. He had already formulated plans to go into the security business in the D.C. area following his retirement from the Air Force.

Sergeant Johnson was armed with a military issue 9mm Beretta semi-automatic handgun and an M-16 assault-rifle. What he could accomplish with these Twentieth Century weapons in a future, possibly hostile environment, he could only speculate, with some concern. Norm would joke about this with his fellow crew members:

"I can see myself stepping out of our little elevator with these weapons and immediately getting zapped by a purple ray and turned into an oversized rabbit... Don't laugh—they might turn you guys into penguins."

*   *   *

Following another movie, on their fourth night in space, the crew sat around the nine foot diameter table at the center of the cabin and began their usual evening chat. They sat on the table's tall chairs that resembled comfortable bar stools with arm rests and padded seats. The table top was four and one half feet above the smooth deck; this height allowed for the easy access to the elevator hatch which was located just below. In order to egress the ship, each crew member had to grasp the overhead handles which were attached to the underside overhang of the table. They would then swing themselves down through the hatch into the crew elevator. The below table hatch opened towards the rear of the ship and just beyond this was the elaborate calisthenics machine and work-out station.

Each crewmember was required to spend one hour a day going through a series of pre-programmed exercise routines. This was normally accomplished in two separate half-hour sessions. Just beyond this station was the nine foot wide, very well appointed galley. This location took up a small portion of the inner circumference of the cabin. The five crew bunks were also in this ring along with the two bathrooms, or "crew heads" as they were referred to.

On the other side of the central table, along the ship's inner-circumference, was the sixteen foot wide control panel. This is where the five crew stations were located with their fixed padded swivel based crew seats. It was here where the glowing displays of the control consoles added orange highlights to the often intense expressions of the crewmembers. Just above these panels were the three forty inch wide forward view screens. These gave the crew a clear view of the heavens, now streaked with patterns of light in various shades of subtle colors, representing the stars and planets of the limitless universe.

Beyond this seventy-two foot circumference of the inner cabin limits, was a seven foot wide band which included the control mechanisms, the crew-head fixtures, crew bunks and crew storage, and the appliances of the galley. Then beyond this ring, extending outward to the edge of the ship, was the intricate propulsion mechanism. This took up the last ten feet of the ship's diameter and ended with the four foot thick glowing projection belt. This anti-matter powered drive mechanism occupied the entire outer ring which had a circumference of one hundred and seventy-nine feet at its outer edge.

As the crew now sat around the large round table at the center of their colorfully painted control room, Rob attempted to answer Lilly's questions about the drive system.

"I really don't understand it myself Red."

"Boy—that's really reassuring Rob, seeing that you're the Flight Engineer on this bus," came Lilly's immediate response.

"Let me give it a try Red," continued Rob.

"This drive system is referred to as 'Magnetic Impulse Projection Warp Drive.' It utilizes an extremely high-energy series of impulses which were used to project it to an electrically designated target. We have to set a specific target cross-section into the computer's three dimensional space grid and then energize the magnetic impulse drive at a pre-designated power, which then projects its beam from the outer edge of our disc."

"We're in a circular orbit right now Rob," responded Lilly. "How can we set a specific projection target while we're spinning around the earth?"

Janet picked up on the question and responded to Lilly's remark.

"Red—our projected target is ourselves. That's how we can establish a circular course. Actually, it's an elliptical course because of the earth's solar orbit."

"I get it!" added Norm. "We're chasing ourselves around the earth as the earth chases itself around the Sun. Just saying this makes me dizzy. Is that right guys?"

"You got it Norm," cut in Boss. "We're simply trying to fly up our own six."

The entire crew got a laugh out of this remark which referred to the clock position used by fliers. "Six o'clock" was simply the ships or, in this case, a human's backside. The tiny crew continued with their amusing comments as their glowing space ship sped on with increased purpose.

*　　*　　*

Soon the courageous crew members were in their final day of earth orbit. Janet trained her heavily filtered tracking scope once more on the sun. Their great spinning orbit remained on a plain that held the Astronomical Unit, (a.u.) at a 93 million mile constant in relationship to the sun. They were orbiting the sun as a satellite of their home planet, thereby continuously intersecting earth's solar orbit.

Following a few more minutes of study and timing checks, Jan turned towards Major Brice and began to discuss her recent findings. The other crew members turned their chairs in order to watch and hear the exchange. They all felt that their was obvious concern in Jan's remarks.

"Boss! You know that when we studied the sun's Chromosphere and Corona in real time, the main features, including the sun spots, were fixed and we only saw the changes on 'time-lapsed' still exposures taken hours and often even days apart."

"Right Jan. I suppose that you can see the movement of the main flares now that we are in a different time continuum—correct?"

"Yes Boss, but it's not simply movement of the flares, the sun seems to be boiling! I was watching the movement of the photosphere and trying to time it's revolutions in relationship to the same studies I made from earth. I know that you are aware that the photosphere makes a full three hundred and sixty degree revolution every twenty seven days of earth time. It now seems to be completing a revolution about every three hundred and twenty seconds."

"My God—you must have made an error Janet. That doesn't seem possible. What does that math out to be as far as our *time-jump* ratio?"

Major Brice was trying to inquire in a subdued tone, however, it was apparent to the crew that his interest in Captain Hulse's findings had become intense.

"We seem to be moving through decades of earth time. One of our days on this ship may be equivalent to seven or even eight thousand days on earth. It seems to math out as seventy-four hundred to one."

Major Brice stared at Captain Hulse without speaking. Sergeant Lilly French raised her hand calculator and excitedly announced:

"That's over twenty years per day! We're completing our final day at speed in just a few hours. Your calculations Jan put us back on earth between one-hundred and one-hundred and ten years in the future. We're going to return to earth in the Twenty-Second Century. All our family and friends will be gone!"

"Now hold on Red, and the rest of you as well. These calculations could be faulty. How certain are you about this Jan?"

"I'm not certain Boss. It could easily be some unknown perceptual effect caused by our speed, however I'm certain of my original time frames on earlier sun studies. I believe that I recorded them accurately."

"Well, everyone stay calm… We'll be starting our slow-down and instrument checks for reentry, shortly."

* * *

In 1984 Lilly "Red" French was born and spent the early years of her life in the old Long Island whaling village of Sag Harbor. The town had, in recent years, become quite well known throughout the country. It was considered part of the affluent summer resort area known as "The Hamptons." In fact it was surrounded by South Hampton, Bridgehampton and East Hampton. These four villages, along with Watermill, Sagaponic and Amaganset, located on the eastern end of Long Island, New York, had long since become a summer playground for the stars, as well as the very wealthy.

Lilly's family were far from famous, but they had been successful "Ship-Wrights" dating back to the glory days of mid-Nineteenth Century whaling. It was the "French" family that had built many of the fine old homes in Sag Harbor, including the famous Whaling Museum. Lilly's parents were well educated and cultured people. The family prided itself on having good style and taste when it came to the arts. This was passed on to Lilly and her two brothers as well. Her brother David was a successful attorney in New Haven, Connecticut, while her brother John was an equally successful surgeon living in Vermont.

Lilly had entered Rhode Island School of Design in Providence in 2002. She only spent two terms at this fine school of art and design before she realized that she suffered from a form of red-green color blindness. She then joined the Air Force and studied photography.

As a cameraman the colors of life were fixed, and as long as she stayed away from the color processing and printing end of the business, she could effectively use her artistic flair. Lilly was a fine sketch artist. She also had become an accomplished photographer, which is why she was chosen as a member of this tiny crew. She was ordered to photographically document their adventure.

Lilly was a pretty young woman with her dark red hair and light skin. She had sparkling green eyes and penetrating gaze. She had never married and wasn't overly worried about her "biological clock." She was still in her twenties and was in no hurry to walk down the proverbial aile. She, also had a couple of jealous boyfriends whom didn't really appreciate, yet grudgingly tolerated the arrangement. Lilly did possess the quick temper that those with her physical characteristics had become, often incorrectly, known for. Her family name and ancestry was derived from the little children of the French nobility that were sent to America to escape the "Guillotine" during the French Revolution. It seems that a few Irish and Dutch ladies had slipped into the lineage, hence her red hair and fair skin.

Lilly "Red" French at 5'9" tall, fell just inside the height limitations for crew members on this mission. Unlike the more diminutive Janet, this athletic young woman was a tall, statuesque, striking member of the crew. Janet Hulse's beauty was remarkable, however Lilly was also beautiful. The male crew members considered themselves lucky to have such good looking female companions. The three male members all came to the conclusion that this must have been an unwritten requirement by the senior board that selected the final crew.

To carry out her assignment as the mission photographer, Lilly brought two digital cameras with her in a compact leather carrying case. One was a small 8.2 mega-pixel Cannon which she used for her candid shots, and it seemed to the rest of the crew that she always had this camera at the ready, yet often out of sight. She was like a magician, producing this fine little gadget at just the right, or arguably, the wrong moment. The other camera was a larger 12.1 mega-pixel Pentax which was primarily a motion-picture camera. These cameras were also capable of extreme zoom ranges and exposure possibilities. Between the two cameras and the computer printer that she had at her console, Lilly was able to supply a seemingly endless number of 4"X 6" photographs for her appreciative crew mates.

* * *

The descent back to low earth orbit went without incident and was accomplished in the projected time frame. They were all apprehensive concerning what they might find as they returned to their home. *Were Jan and Red's calculations correct?* This question pervaded everyone's thoughts as they approached their spinning home planet.

As they decelerated, Major Brice repeatedly attempted to raise their home-base "Prickly Peak" on the secure channel they were assigned. There was no response so he switched to open frequencies. The speaker was clicked into the intercom and they all heard the music. None of them knew the tunes that were coming in over the ships speakers. The sounds were deep and melodious like classical music, yet unrecognizable. Red knew the classics as well as anyone on the crew, but she simply shook her head.

Tom Brice then moved the dial once more, and this brought an unintelligible string of code spewing from the speakers. He turned the volume down and continued searching. Finally came the singing voices. As the crew listened intently, they looked from one to the other with equally quizzical expression.

"What language is that!"

Norm searched the others for a response.

"It sounds like Spanish or wait… It's Italian," Jan interjected.

"That's what it is," added Lilly. "It's Grand Opera, *Puccini*. Nothing new about that."

They continued circling the globe until they were in a holding position at 120,000 feet altitude over the western coast of the United States. At this point Janet attempted to get a visual of Vandenberg Air Force Base, their designated secondary landing site. She focused her scope and then instructed "Boss" to maneuver to specific coordinates.

"We should be well above any commercial air traffic at this altitude, so we had better hold our position and try to determine just what's going on down there."

Major Brice solemnly addressed his tiny crew with these facts, then continued:

"We're not getting any communication indicators from our home-base. Our secondary landing site is your base Rob. We are now interrupting communications originating at Vandenberg."

The others could here the drone of what seemed to be military jargon coming from their speakers. The fact that it was in English was reassuring to all.

"That enormous runway they have there should still be operational even if a century has passed, not that we need a runway with this ship. However, it will make it possible to land well away from any buildings or possibly unfriendly reception committees. Naturally, I'll try to make radio communication prior to landing."

"It's a good choice boss. They have very little air traffic there. At least that was the case when I left last year—or should I say last century."

Vandenberg Air Force Base was the vast Western Test Range located on California's Central Coast. It covered more than one hundred and fifty square miles including 43 miles of the scenic Pacific Coast.

"Vandenberg it is then!"

Major Tom "Boss" Brice made this fateful statement as he entered the giant base's coordinates into his softly glowing console.

# CHAPTER FOUR

Following instructions from the Vandenberg Flight Control Tower, Major Brice prepared to land AG-1 at the northwestern end of the 18,000 foot long runway. He had been directed to descend from altitude just off California's rocky coast, opposite the base. He was then instructed to proceed inland at a 3,000 foot altitude and land at a predetermined spot some distance from Base Operations.

As they slid over the coast on an easterly heading, Rob Carmody studied the familiar scene. However, it wasn't familiar at all.

"My God! What happened to Santa Maria?"

The medium sized Central California coastal city of approximately 100,000 souls had grown well beyond what he could have imagined. The city now had a sky-line that stretched across the forward view screens, just beyond the limits of the base. The new city seemed to center just south of old Santa Maria where the little town of Orcutt had been and on down to southeast through an area where the renowned Central Coast grape vineyards had rolled across the low lying hills. This land was more elevated than the original location of the Santa Maria Valley. Rob looked to his left and noticed a blue reflection coming up from where Guadalupe and the original low-lying city of Santa Maria had been located.

"Look at that sky-line… Santa Maria had only a few tall buildings and they're gone. It's as if the entire city has been moved south and grown—really grown! I just can't believe it!"

Rob's emotional reaction surprised the entire crew. Each of them now began to fully realize that they really had made an enormous time-jump. They looked at one another in total amazement. Here was the truth, dramatically spread out right below and in front of them. Here was the reality; no longer was it just speculative theory.

*    *    *

The apprehensive crewmembers remained quietly inside their space-ship following their successful landing, in compliance with instructions from the Vandenberg tower. They were told that a medical team would come out and inspect them, as well as their ship. This was normal procedure for anyone coming in from a space journey, so no one onboard found this unusual. What they all did find unusual, however, was the vehicle that brought the medical team out to the end of the runway.

It was a very sleek, rather small bus painted in Air Force Blue with the usual white identification numerals and "U.S. Aerospace Service" printed in white letters on the front door panels. What was different was that the little bus had no wheels or wheel wells. It seemed to glide along a foot or two above the rough terrain, not needing taxi strips, roads or even paths.

"It seems that 'Anti-grav' has really taken over. We're not the only ones; it's become a success."

Major Brice made this statement, then remarked:

"Good news… There's still an Air Force or should I now say 'Aerospace Service', and even more important—there's still a United States."

Four personnel in pale green "Hazmat Suits" jumped from the hovering vehicle and one of them signaled for the crew to lower the elevator. The crew of AG-1 also heard this instruction over their intercom along with the following:

"Welcome home Major Brice and Crew! We've been expecting you for quite awhile. With your permission, we'll come aboard for a brief medical check and then we will accompany you all on over to Flight Operations."

"Permission granted!"

Major Brice's response was swift and military. There was no further verbal exchange between the medical team, with their heads covered with antibacterial hoods, and the five members of the AG-1 crew.

Following the brief medical checks, which were accomplished with electronic scanning devices, they were all invited aboard the strange, quietly hovering, little blue bus. Then the officer in charge of the medical team stated in a flat voice:

"R-Seven, return to Operations Sector One."

The driver-less vehicle responded immediately and sped off towards Operations. During the drive in, the crew noticed many odd shaped, including some saucer shaped, aircraft parked across the enormous tarmac. Some rested on conventional landing gear and others on elaborate permanent stands. A few were extremely large and Major Brice estimated the diameter of these disc shaped spacecraft to be in excess of 200 feet. There was some observable air traffic as a few conventional aircraft were waiting their turn to take off. Major Brice also noticed a few flashes of light at altitude, and deduced that these aircraft were equipped with anti-collision "Repulse-Radar" systems.

On the trip into base operations each member of the medical team shed their bio-protective suits and placed them in containers in the back of the bus. The astronauts didn't notice anything unusual about these individuals as their primary interest was outside the tinted windows of the vehicle.

Base Operations was housed in an enormous concrete and glass building and the adjacent control tower reached some twenty stories into the clear mid-afternoon sky. As they neared the ramp entrance in front of the impressive building, Brice's crew were all surprised to see a large group of people stretching out towards them from the buildings entrance. They seemed to have been formed into some sort of a welcoming committee.

"How did they know we were coming? I thought we had communications blackout. How could they tell the precise time? Maybe this reception is for someone else? I thought that this was a secret mission. What's going on?"

These questions, and more, were whispered back and forth by the five startled space travelers. The shocks were coming quickly now as they stepped down from their transport which was now sitting solidly on its short landing struts. The five astronauts were then led up a long and neatly rolled out red carpet by the medical officer in charge of the arrival team.

"We've been monitoring your orbit for quite a few years and we then timed your slowing and descent for the past few months. We knew you would come here to your secondary landing assignment because your primary base at Cactus Peak no longer exists."

The colonel in charge of the medical team offered this information when he noticed the quizzical murmuring among the members of the AG-1 crew.

* * *

As they walked across the ramp leading to the entrance of the Operations Building, the uniformed personnel came to attention while a large mass of civilians crowded the control lines and cheered. The crew were surprised and amused by the reception. Many of the civilians raised there small digital cameras to arms reach above their heads in order to photograph the five space travelers.

Rob noticed a young child in the front row, who was pointing at them with a puzzled expression. Then the child's mother pushed his arm down and shook her finger at him. It was then that he realized that he and the rest of his crew were different. He looked more closely at the cheering crowd and a faint chill of alarm flickered up his spine.

*Had the others noticed?* he wondered.

He turned towards Major Brice who immediately nodded, as if to say:

*Yes Rob, I see.*

There were no white people in the crowd or among the airmen still standing smartly at attention. There were no Blacks, Asians or Hispanics, either.

"That's why they're all staring at us—while taking pictures and cheering," whispered Major Brice in Rob's ear.

Rob slowed his pace and studied the crowd more closely. What he now saw was as amazing to him as it was to the rest of the crew. These individuals that surround them, had beautiful smooth golden toned skin. Most of them had varying shades of primarily dark hair except for the obvious older gray haired individuals. There were no blonds in the crowd and all seemed to enjoy the same bronze complexion. They all seemed to be tall and slender and quite handsome with their fine facial features. Rob noticed that all of the women seemed very beautiful, yet these people were not clones. On closer inspection, he could easily see that their individual facial characteristics were different. Although they were tall, there still was a noticeable variance in their heights. Rob roughly figured that the men seemed to average about 6' 2" tall, and the attractive women must have been nearer to 5' 8" in average height. As these tall slender, striking individuals continued to welcome the crew members, Rob thought, almost comically:

*My God! They must have emptied out all the Hollywood studios and modeling agencies to come up with this crowd. Christ—maybe they are aliens from another world?*

As they continued on toward the entrance, the excited crew members, almost simultaneously, noticed the large banner unfurled above the heavy glass doors.

**WELCOME HOME TIME TRAVELERS---**
**WELCOME TO THE <u>FOURTH</u> MILLENNIUM**

An older uniformed individual stepped forward as the even more startled crew entered the spacious building. The five came smartly to attention and saluted the blue uniformed four star general. Their short periods of non-military informality were suddenly over.

"Welcome aboard Colonel Brice," said the general.

"Thank you General—but I'm a major Sir!"

"Not now Colonel… You've *all* been promoted one grade—you are now Lieutenant Colonel Thomas Brice. I feel that this is the least that we can do seeing that you all have at least one thousand and seventeen years in grade."

This resulted in a big laugh among the senior officials in attendance.

The crew of AG-1 turned towards one another in astonishment. They now realized that the banner was correct, and that they hadn't spent a hundred years of earth time in their little ship; a thousand years had passed since they left the parched Nevada Desert.

"That makes this year *Three Thousand and Thirty!* Is that correct Sir?"

Janet Hulse fired off the question that they all had been wanting to ask since landing.

General Kincaid, Aerospace Service Chief of Staff, studied his watch and said:

"That's right *Major* Hulse— It's Fifteen-Twenty-Five hours on the Sixteenth of April in the year Three Thousand and Thirty. You have just entered the Fourth Millennium."

Janet turned to her newly promoted boss and said:

"Please forgive me, aah, Colonel Brice, Sir… I must have missed placed a decimal point when I gave the time ratio to Technical, or should I now say, Master Sergeant French. It was seventy-four *thousand* to one—not seventy-four hundred to one. Just a minor mistake, right!," added the obviously chagrined officer.

"No problem Major Hulse. Your math had no effect on our trip because we were in the count-down for descent at that time anyway. The way it looks around here, we may have unconsciously picked a pretty good time to come back."

With this said, Lieutenant Colonel Tom Brice turned to the general and said:

"Thank you Sir! Thank you for this warm reception. We had no idea what to expect when we arrived, especially after determining that we had made a significant time-jump. What are our orders now General Kincaid?"

* * *

The crew of AG-1 were ordered to remain in Operations for debriefing. The debriefing, they were told, would take about an hour, while their update briefing would take at least a week. It would require this much time because it would include an historical update on what had transpired during the past millennium. This would require more than one instructor, and a good deal of classroom time.

*Senior* Master Sergeant Rob Carmody asked a rather pertinent question when being informed of this plan:

"How come the language hasn't deteriorated, or at least significantly changed, during such an extended period of time?"

Captain Driscoll, their newly assigned guide and liaison officer, responded:

"It seems that the television and radio network executives, in an attempt to employ announcers and analysts that spoke *proper* English, have helped, although indirectly, to preserve the language. That, of course is the spoken language. The real protection has come from the editors of books and periodicals and the elementary, middle and high schools, as well as the universities that educated these editors along with the rest of us. The object during the past few centuries was to hold the line against the influx of slang and coarseness. Actually, they have managed quite well except for some rather glaring failures that you will probably notice. And—yes, we still have television although it may be a little more three dimensional than you remember. We'll be going over all of this during your briefings."

Captain Mathias Driscoll was going to be their primary contact with this new world. He had majored in Military History prior to his commissioning. When he was informed, three months earlier, that he was picked to take on this task, he concentrated his research on general, less specific, history of the late Twentieth and early Twenty-First Centuries. Mathias was typical of the people that greeted the space travelers. He stood 6' 4" tall, board shouldered and quite handsome with his deep-set eyes and muscular jaw. Even more important, he seemed good natured, with a sense of humor that would be necessary as the inevitable questions continued. He was finally able to maneuver the crew away from the reception committee and into a nearby vacant office.

"Even the uniforms and insignia seem very similar to ours," said *Master* Sergeant Norman Johnson after taking a seat along with his comrades.

"Are the ranks and insignia the same?"

"Pretty much," replied Driscoll.

"What about money? What do you use for money? Do you owe us a thousand years of back pay…?

This last question came from a now grinning Norman Johnson.

"We couldn't afford to pay you that much money, Sergeant Johnson. You all will be paid for six days in space even though you only completed five— how's that Sergeant?"

The captain flashed an evil grin with this reply, after watching a few jaws drop.

"Just kidding Sergeant. However, money is totally different now and all that will be explained in greater detail during the week of briefings. In the meantime, each of you will be issued debit cards with two-thousand 'Megas' of credits which should be sufficient to hold you until we get your new pay straightened out. We no longer use currency."

Tom Brice looked at the young captain and said, "Megas, no currency?"

"Yes Sir Colonel, regular dollars are long gone. Enough questions for now, if you please. Let me try and get you all situated. I've sent some airmen out to pick up your belongings."

The five space travelers were then introduced to Doctor Marian Kozak who had just entered the office. Marian Kozak immediately offered them coffee and doughnuts which were conveniently spread out on a folding table near a broad window on the west side of the room. Major Kozak, another very attractive woman, then had them all take a seat and proceeded to ask questions about their five day mission. Normally debriefings such as this were handled one on one. In this rather unique situation Doctor Kozak directed her questions toward newly promoted Tom Brice, after indicating that their responses were being recorded. The first questions simply covered the operation of the ship, and any possible malfunctions. Then came the questions to everyone concerning psychological impacts on the crew members as they began to realize the effects of the time-jump.

"Colonel Brice, when did you realize that you had moved through a millennium in just five days?"

"Just now Doctor. We just became aware of this out in the lobby here. Actually, when we saw that welcoming banner over the entrance. We knew we had jumped more than they warned us, a few hours before landing, but we thought it was a century, not a thousand years."

"How does that make you feel now Colonel?"

"Of course we were shocked by this when we thought it was a century instead of a few months or a year or two, as was predicted. When I saw that banner at the entrance, I realized that it had been a millennium. My thought then was, a century—a millennium, what's the difference? All of our acquaintances were gone—so what the hell's the difference?"

"What about the rest of you?" was the doctor's next question.

The responses were similar as she made eye contact with each crew member, in an attempt to elicit the true emotional response from each. Marian Kozak then added:

"It's best that you all landed when you did. If, in fact, you had landed a century after taking off, you would have arrived during a disastrous period in this planet's history. The other briefings will get into this subject in much more detail."

The doctor continued with the debriefing until the five and a half day flight experience had been fully explored. Marian Kozak was a trained Aerospace Service psychologist, a fact which she eventually informed the group. She also explained that she was searching for any clues to serious emotional disturbances that might have arisen among the crew following their historic flight. She continued with her questioning for some time. Some of the questions were rhetorical and some were individual. Doctor Kozak then introduced a subject that she felt might test the astronauts psychological stability:

"I want to explain to you all how we deal with elderly nursing home patients whom have been certified as 'Terminal.' I have learned that you come from an era that continued to medicate and even perform surgeries on these patients. The medical approach in your day was to prolong their lives even when your care-givers were fully aware that these patients were miserable, or only semi-conscious, even unconscious. Once an elderly patient's prognosis is classified as terminal, only pain relieving medicines are administered and no surgeries are allowed. We no longer have incapacitated elderly patients suffering in nursing homes for extended periods."

Colonel Brice spoke up following this statement: "Doctor Kozak—by the time we left on this mission, this also had become the accepted practice in this country. Therefore, I don't think that there is much shock effect in your statement, if indeed that's what you were trying for Major."

"Very good Colonel, however let me now add the clincher. I believe that you all are aware of the term *euthanasia*. The pain relieving medicines are administered for only a limited time, that is, time enough to make a final prognosis. Then the patient is either placed on a prescribed road to recovery or chemically terminated. It is now the medical practice to terminate terminally ill patients following a detailed official medical board review of their case.

This brought her an immediate easily discernible response from the crew members.

"Sounds like the vindication of Doctor Kevorkian—finally!"

Lilly French's response was immediate yet she wasn't sure if Major Kozak had ever heard of the courageous doctor.

Janet Hulse merely shook her head slowly and with a rather puzzled expression.

"Yes Sergeant French we know about Doctor Kevorkian, and that's what I was trying for and that's what I just now received—your reaction! Also—I would like to know if any of you feel that this is an improper way to treat terminally ill patients. Further, I'm trying to spot any serious problems that any of you might have that could conflict with your individual upbringing, when concerned with religion. Now, what are your answers to this?"

Rob Carmody responded to this slowly and with emotion:

"How can any individual take on such a responsibility as the termination of a human life? Especially a doctor who has taken the Hippocratic oath? That's God's work Major. That's the Lords decision when a human must die."

"Sergeant Carmody… We now believe that God would want us to make this determination on our own. It has to do with human suffering and we believe that God really is benevolent."

Tom Brice then asked: "How long Doctor? How long following the initial prognosis of terminal illness does a medical board make its determination?"

"It's pretty quick Colonel. Naturally it varies with each case, but in all these cases it doesn't exceed a few hours, often the administration of the necessary drugs is immediately following the final decision to terminate. Remember we are dealing with patients who are in continuous pain, semi-conscious, or who are totally unconscious at best."

Each member of the crew, including Sergeant Carmody, then gave the inquisitive young doctor a somewhat positive response to this practice, with some natural religion based reservations. There were a few more questions about this now accepted practice of euthanasia, which Doctor Kozak answered precisely, then all was quiet.

Following this and after determining that the entire crew seemed to be mentally well adjusted despite their recent traumatic experiences in space, she made her final pronouncement:

"I feel that all of you have adjusted to this rather amazing 'time-jump' extremely well. I'm going to give all of you a clean bill of health, at least as far as your psychological profiles are concerned. I don't believe any of you are dangerously psychotic or clinically insane, but, I could be wrong—so beware—I'll be watching…!"

This last remark, spoken with a smile, brought the intended amused response.

* * *

The giant operations complex also included Visiting Aircrew Quarters, along with an old fashioned cafeteria, a coffee shop, and a much needed cocktail lounge. Vandenberg also had a large Base Exchange just a few miles away and a Uniform Sales Outlet in the same area. There was an enormous base housing complex, athletic fields and Elementary, Middle, and High Schools for the children of the approximately thirty thousand uniformed and civilian personnel stationed at the giant base. To be assigned as Permanent-Party at Vandenberg was considered a reward. Blessed with some of the best weather on the planet, California's Central Coast was still one of *the* places to live.

Vandenberg was the home of the Marshallia Ranch Golf Course, which had been listed as one of the best military golf courses in the nation. During their landing, golfer Rob Carmody had noticed that this beautiful course was still there just north of the business center of the base. At the time of their landing he was pleased that it had lasted through the century, and now he was astounded that it was still there, green and plush after a thousand years. He decided that he would drag Norm out there when they got the chance. He was convinced that Norm was no Tiger Woods, as he had said. For that matter, thought Rob, who was? Rob knew that Norm was a fine athlete and that he probably was a very competent golfer.

Each crew member now came to the realization that this would be their home for some time. They were also aware that a visit into the giant city directly to their east, would require some extensive briefing on modern customs and practices. To a person, they were relieved that they didn't have to enter this new civilian world before being re-educated. Therefore they all looked forward to the briefings that Matt

Driscoll had indicated that they would receive in the coming days. Their enthusiasm was somewhat subdued with thoughts concerned with what kind of a new world lay out there beyond the guarded gates of Vandenberg Air Service Base. Each member of the crew was now coming to the sober realization that there really was no going back. There was no return from this extraordinary trip. To the crew it was like that old philosophical chestnut, "*there's no going home.*"

# CHAPTER FIVE

After having been assigned individual rooms and then unpacking their meager belongings, the crew assembled in the large Flight Operations coffee shop.

"Not much has changed in coffee shops," said Rob, after looking around the well appointed room. "However—I don't see any grill. It must be behind the counter or in the back. I certainly don't smell any grease either—a good thing."

"What's to change?" Norm responded:

"A coffee shop is a coffee shop, right?"

There were red padded booths along the colorfully decorated walls, and matching red padded bar stools set up along a curved granite counter. The red material looked like Twentieth Century naugahyde, yet as they took their seats they found it to be far more supple and the plush padding was surprisingly comfortable. A young civilian lady dressed in tan slacks and a form fitting white jacket greeted the "Five" politely. She led them to a large booth situated below a broad window that overlooked the aircraft parking ramp on the west side of the building. Norm Johnson pointed to the scene beyond the window and remarked:

"Look at how clear and warm it is out there. They tell us that it's mid-April and yet it was actually very pleasant out there on the tarmac. The air is so clear—it must have something to do with controlling the atmosphere. Maybe they have finally learned to clean the air."

"This is the Central Coast of California Norm," replied Rob Carmody. "The late afternoons in this part of California are normally like this during the spring, and actually most of the time. It's about seventy out there right now—maybe sixty-eight. It's the 'Marine Layer,' some fog in the morning and like this in the afternoon. This keeps the temperatures under control throughout the day. There is a coastal strip of this kind of weather running from Monterrey down to Ventura. That is where the temperatures in this, approximately twelve to fifteen mile wide coastal band, are like we've seen here today. Go East just beyond this area and the temperatures this time of year, may go up as much as twenty degrees. For many years, this Central Coast climate was a well kept secret, however, judging by the size of that city rising to the east—the word is out."

"You really liked being stationed here, didn't you Rob?"

Norm's question received a positive shake of the head from a wistful Rob Carmody.

There were only a few other individuals in the coffee shop at this time and they were dressed in military flight suits. They smiled then whispered to one another, as they stared, almost rudely, at the five time-travelers who were dressed in their $21^{st}$ Century civilian clothes.

Lilly "Red" French looked intently at the pleasant young woman who was now waiting on their table. Lilly felt a quick chill down her spine, then asked if she could take her picture with her ever present little digital camera. The smiling young waitress was willing and Lilly promised her a print as soon as she could get to her computer and return.

*This woman*, she thought silently, *is obviously working at this low wage job, yet she seems very friendly and she's gorgeous. Her complexion seems perfect—not a blemish. What chance do I have in this new society with my plain looks?*

Lilly was far from plain but suffered from the doubts that many athletic young women have concerning their appearance. She would soon find out that her light skin and dark red hair would be a boon, instead of a detriment.

* * *

The following morning, the five AG-1 crew members met in a large, well-appointed office on the third floor of the operations complex.

Captain Mathias Driscoll warmly welcomed them, then indicated the location of the little coffee bar set-up in the far corner. This was to be an informal opening to their introduction into their new world. Captain Driscoll started the proceedings by saying:

"As you all may have noticed, much has changed in the past thousand years, yet—surprisingly, much has not. First, this is now Vandenberg Air Service Base named for the former Air Force Chief of Staff, General Hoyt S. Vandenberg. We now call our bases 'Air Service' bases because 'Aerospace Service Base' doesn't quite make it, and we don't use the word 'Force' in the titles any longer. Now let's get to the subject at hand, along with a little touch of history.

As you well educated individuals are undoubtedly aware, the thousand years *prior* to your own births encompassed staggering changes as humans moved from the 'Dark' then 'Middle-ages' on into the 'Renaissance. Then came the 'Industrial Age' and finally to what you folks naturally considered to be 'Modern-times.' Your *modern times* are what we now refer to as the 'World War Period.' During that Second Millennium that preceded you, we saw many changes in nations and languages. It was also a period of religious suppression of intellectual thought. National borders changed dramatically. With the Renaissance, the restraints of the great religions finally began to ease and a world of science and true logic began to develop. Since that time, logic and scientific discover have continued without the artificial restraints of ancient religious doctrine."

With this last statement, some of the crew members twisted uneasily in their comfortable chairs. Janet Hulse wondered silently to herself:

"Have I just entered an Atheistic Society?"

Driscoll continued, however, he was aware of the anxiety of some members of the crew.

"We still have religions, churches and services, and the services are very well attended. However religious doctrine has been modified and fanatical behavior has all but been eliminated. For any modern religion to claim that they are, 'the only true faith,' is no longer acceptable. The term 'modern religions' still refers to many of the old religions, now with somewhat modified teachings. We feel that the spiritual world is all around us but most of us now sense that in the past none of the great religions had gotten *it* quite right. In their efforts to control a willing and pliable mass of parishioners they needed to claim that they were the only true faith. They needed to do this back in the years of superstition, but eventually this tactic didn't work.

"As I'm sure that all of you are aware, this was often the instigator of wars an unrest back in your era. However, no one here denies the great good done by most religious organizations and that is one of the reasons why they are still popular and effective. We all now accept *all* major religions. There is also a growing realization that most of them are correct about the *after-life*, and when one departs this life their awareness or essence will go into the portion of the spiritual world that is compatible with each persons particular belief.

"Whoa! I can see by your expressions that this is a new revelation and somewhat alien to your present beliefs."

"Seems a little radical Captain!" exclaimed Tom Brice.

"I'm sure it does Sir, however—and let me make this point perfectly clear. 'Hell' has been removed from religion. It is no longer needed to keep a submissive parish. It is now felt that no 'Benevolent God' could be so sadistic as to condemn a soul, with the faults and limitations supposedly imposed by that same deity, to the anguish of an eternal hell. For example, you cannot condemn a mentally ill, or unstable individual for his irrational behavior. You can remove him from the public, or *reprogram* his brain, but even our Gods cannot remand this individual to unspeakable agony. This is the infusion of syllogistic logic into religious doctrine. The 'Heaven' portion of religious doctrine is still under scrutiny."

"*Reprogram!*" Tom Brice's response was quick and sharp.

"We have acquired the skill to reprogram recessive, or what we refer to as dangerously anti-social brain patterns. This will be discussed in greater detail—later."

Matt Driscoll looked at each of his doubting pupils separately as he made his point. Although he was younger in biological age than all the crew members and held an inferior military grade to Brice and Hulse; he showed them all only small deference. He was very polite in his presentation, but left no question concerning who was in-charge of their little briefing.

"There have been no wars now for nearly a thousand years," continued the tall articulate officer. "Most of the root causes have long since disappeared. Natural disasters have supplanted the illogical competitive desires of mankind to be superior and controlling in their dealings with one-another. Great wealth is frowned upon, as is any ostentation. We shall discuss in detail these disasters and how they eventually brought the human race together.

"As you have probably guessed by now, the '*race-card*' has long since been played out. There is only one human race, and no—we're not a conquering race of space travelers that have taken over your planet."

Rob smiled at this remark, and thought to himself:

*I wasn't really serious when I thought of such a possibility.*

"I am a mixture of you," continued Captain Driscoll. "I am you—and every other race that this planet held forty generations ago. It all began back in your centuries as the ease of mobility increased with air travel. Also, your world wars helped spread the seed. You sent your young soldiers throughout the world, as did many other nations. That's when it really began in earnest. This then, is where the age old problems of racial and ethnic hatreds began to retreat. The intermixing of the races and ethnic groups had begun in earnest. It had started in earlier centuries, but air travel really speeded it up. Religious intolerance was a tougher nut to crack. However, I digress. It still was the huge natural disasters, following your time, that really brought mankind together. We all had a common cause and our previous differences soon became looked upon as foolish, although devastating diversions. Man had found new causes to focus his survival based emotional fury upon."

Driscoll once more individually eyed his intrigued little audience and said:

"As I'm certain you all are aware, famous quotes from different historic figures get passed down through the ages. Your Twentieth Century is no exception. Certainly we've retained famous lines from Franklin Roosevelt's, Jack Kennedy's, Martin Luther King and Ronald Reagan's speeches, as well as many others. Yet one of the most enduring quotes from your era is Rodney King's: '*Can't we all—just get along?*' It was a rather articulate assessment of the human condition, from a rather bewildered yet perceptive, unfortunate."

The crew all shook their heads in the affirmative, for they were all aware of that event.

The smiling captain picked up a small black object similar to a TV remote control device. He then aimed the device at the far wall. The wall seemed to open up into a three dimensional display, and although it was merely a sophisticated form of holographic projection, for the next ninety minutes his enthralled audience watched an impressive show depicting the subject of racial integration and mixing. Charts, diagrams and cartoon characters were employed in instructing the crew members in how the stronger DNA, was allowed to take over which resulted in the eventual strengthening of the human genome and epi-genome, as well as some subtle scientific engineering of this delicate genome structure. They were also informed of the life expectancy of humans and how it had increased dramatically in the very recent past. They were told that it had dropped significantly during some of the "Dark Periods" endured during the early portion of the third millennium. They were somewhat startled when the production indicated that one's life expectancy had recently passed the 120 year mark for both men and women. This was graphically illustrated with the section on fourth millennium medicine and the final conquest of disease. When the presentation ended Matt Driscoll stood up and stated:

"Your Adolf Hitler had it one hundred and eighty degrees out of phase, when he demanded a pure 'Aryan Race.' He believed that would produce a super race. Eventually, such a course of action, unchecked for just a few generations, would have caused the deterioration of his 'Supermen' into a sickly and intellectually inferior race."

When Matt Driscoll blamed Adolf Hitler on the crew by saying "Your," there was a mumbled negative reaction.

"Sorry... I only meant that concerning your general time period," apologized Driscoll.

"Actually, I am aware that Hitler took his own life long before any of you were born. I do apologize, I realize that he was considered a pariah, even in your time."

Colonel Brice then said: "No problem Captain, but I do have another question about the presentation. There were a couple of instances when our country was referred to as having seventy-one states?"

"Sorry Colonel," replied the tall young officer. "Centuries ago, we annexed old Mexico. Mexico originally had thirty-one states, however, ten were heavily damaged or totally lost to the sea during the time of the disasters. Most of that land has been reclaimed since the 'cooling-period,' however not much permanent structure has been built on these reclaimed lands. They are primarily used for mining and some for agriculture. The state boundaries were redrawn. For that matter, the same thing happened to Florida, yet it remains a separate state. We'll discuss this and other consolidations in up-coming briefings—no time now."

The crew members were wide eyed over this one, then Rob Carmody spoke up:

"What do you mean by saying that we *annexed* old Mexico? What the hell did we do—invade. Did we go to war with Mexico?"

"That wasn't necessary Sergeant Carmody. Our congress passed a resolution of incorporation that was ratified by the states and signed by the President. This was done following a referendum of approval that was made in Mexico. It seems that the citizens of that country were fed up with their politicians and the centuries of poverty that they had promised to correct. Naturally the referendum was not administered by their government. It was initiated by us and their government found itself powerless to prevent it. Their only alternative was to go to war with the United States and that didn't seem like a viable option, even to them."

"I could see it coming… It was the only practical solution. Mexico had great natural resources, but the general population never benefited from these. Annexation was obviously the correct answer to the immigration problem, right?"

"That's correct Sergeant Carmody! There's no poverty anymore."

"Wow—no poverty in old Mexico?" Rob responded quickly to Driscoll's remark.

"No poverty anywhere—worldwide," was the immediate and startling reply.

The rest of the crew joined in on their approval of the annexation and the fact that the annexation took place without a shot being fired.

Matt Driscoll now introduced Major William Hansen to the crew. Hansen was the chief of the Vandenberg weather station. It was Major Hansen who would explain in painful detail, the natural events that nearly ended human occupation of their beautiful blue planet, yet in the end, brought the survivors together in, "True International Harmony."

Major Hanson stood up in front of the group and said:

"It's Eleven-thirty, let's break for lunch, then we can tackle this rather depressing subject on a full stomach. Please try to get back here by One, that should give you a chance to look around the base a little—at least this part of the base. Transportation will be provided for you to both the NCO and Officer's clubs, and being celebrities you can go to either club regardless of your military rank."

* * *

Colonel Brice and Major Hulse accompanied "Bill" Hansen to the "O" Club, where the three sat down in the lounge and enjoyed a beverage before going into the dining room. The lounge was crowded with young officers in uniform. There were a few civilians among them and Janet remarked how little this sort of atmosphere had changed.

"It's only the appearance of the people that has changed. Their behavior seems to be much the same," she mentioned to her companions.

Major Hansen welcomed some of his interested friends over to their table once they had been seated in the large dining room. He turned to his charges and stated:

"I believe Captain Driscoll filled you in on why our appearances have changed somewhat from your century; isn't that so? Here, let me introduce you to these officers."

With this remark Major Hansen stood up and began the introductions. The young officers were very polite and tried to wave the two space travelers back down as they also began to stand. Brice stayed on his feet while Janet sat down as a number of Vandenberg's officer corps lined up at their table. A regular receiving line had now formed as a buzz hummed across the dining hall. The word was out that two of the visitors from the 21$^{st}$ Century were in attendance. There wasn't any overt gawking, however, most of the young men seemed intrigued by the remarkable beauty of Janet Hulse. Even in this era of beautiful people, Janet's magnificent face and form caused a great deal of attention. It was here that Tom Brice began to fully realize his deep feelings for Janet. He could feel an uncomfortable level of jealousy grow and sparkle across his senses as he watched the eyes of the handsome young men taking in the charms of the beautiful woman from the past. He became defensive and whispered to Bill Hansen:

"Enough."

Major Hansen responded immediately and waived off the rest of the well intentioned greeters, saying:

"Thanks for the greetings Gentlemen, thanks so much, but I'm afraid that it is now time for us to get some lunch."

While waiting for their meal, Tom looked around the room and stated:

"I don't see anyone wearing glasses Major."

"Glasses—? Oh, excuse me. You mean eye-glasses? Human vision has been corrected with eye surgery and genome manipulation. Some of these techniques were well on the way to perfection when you left. They'll probably get into that with you all at a later briefing, Colonel Brice."

"No glasses... No glasses world-wide. What about reading glasses Major? What about reading glasses for seniors?"

Not necessary Colonel. I think that you'll both find many of the old human crutches that were so necessary in your time, have disappeared."

"Crutches! I guess that's what they were. What about sun-glasses—you know, shades?"

"You bet Major Hulse. We still have shades... They're part of our style, as I believe they were in your time. I shouldn't say, 'back in your time,' anymore. This now is 'your-time' along with all of us. The Fourth Millennium is *your* millennium!"

* * *

Meanwhile, Rob Carmody, Norm Johnson and Lilly French accompanied Captain Driscoll to the NCO Club. Just before driving them up a hill to the club's entrance, Driscoll said:

"You folks really are celebrities, and as Major Hansen mentioned, we can certainly go to either club and be well received. It's up to you, I'm accompanying you, so hopefully they will let a simple Captain into their NCO Club, if you three decide on this place."

"I think we would feel more comfortable at the NCO Club," responded Senior Master Sergeant Robert Carmody.

This thought was echoed by Sergeants' Johnson and French.

The word was already out when they were about to leave their vehicle. There already were a large number of young men and women, sporting a variety of stripes on their form fitting uniforms, ready to greet them at the front entrance to the impressive club. As the three visitors stepped out of the eerily suspended vehicle, a cheer went up from the greeters. The impromptu cheering continued as they entered the large entrée area. Their tall, handsome, Thirty-first Century hosts were very friendly and quite demonstrative in their enthusiasm.

Their meals were quite good, but it was obvious to the three visitors that they were eating heavily processed foods. As they went through the cafeteria styled food line they all were impressed by the variety of foods on display. And, although the offerings looked just like hamburgers, fish fillets, varying fruits and salads, they tasted a little contrived.

Matt Driscoll informed the three that they were processed and in fact, engineered.

"Much of the harmful ingredients have been removed, and as you probably have noticed, there isn't any obesity among our people. There are other reasons for this as well, and we will be covering this later on in our briefings."

"Sir… Is that just true with the military, or has obesity disappeared in the general population?"

Rob Carmody looked around the dining facility while he asked this question, searching for an overweight person. He didn't see any.

"Not just the military Sergeant, everybody. It's worldwide. Nobody is obese anymore."

The three sergeants laughed at this and then Rob replied:

"You're kidding—aren't you? No poverty worldwide, and now nobody is fat worldwide?"

Matt Driscoll shook his head and with a serious expression continued:

"This also has a lot to do with the improved human genome and the dominant genes that we discussed this morning. The terrific medical costs of obesity, combined with the human suffering it engendered, eventually caused new controls to be put in place. Actually, this occurred centuries ago, and it involved a variety of breakthroughs in animal husbandry and crop engineering. Also, a powerful negative stigma had become attached to obesity until the medical aspects were fully understood. New laws were introduced and obeyed, concerning the distribution of *unhealthy* foods. Our meals may be a little bland when compared with yours, I don't know. I do feel that the present citizens of this planet are healthier."

"Your telling us that everyone complies with these regulations?"

A puzzled Rob Carmody continued:

"Everyone worldwide?"

"I know that this wouldn't have been possible in your time Sergeant," continued Driscoll: "Following the centuries of strengthening of the human genome, compliance became much easier. We all have a strong well balanced metabolism, this combined with our low-fat diet, has actually saved us from obesity. Our low-fat diets do incorporate highly unsaturated fats, which are derived primarily from seed oils. I wouldn't worry about it with you folks. You don't seem to be suffering from this problem and with the foods you'll now have available, well..."

Matt Driscoll looked directly at the shapely Lilly French while making this statement.

"Our food will probably be a big adjustment for you folks. Red meats have been removed from our diet and are no longer available in any form. Those hamburgers listed on the menu are not derived from cattle."

"You mean that there no longer are any cattle ranches...? No slaughter houses? You're telling us that the huge meat-packing industry no longer exists?"

"That industry still exists Rob, but in a much reduced state from what you knew. Part of this is due to the decline in population and part is due to the end of the cattle industry. That industry ended centuries ago during the disasters that Major Hansen will discuss with you following lunch. As I mentioned, no red meats but we still enjoy fish, fowl and of course hogs. I might also add that there no longer is any sports hunting. Fishing yes—hunting no!"

"Good...!" Lilly spoke up, stating that she never did like seeing well provided for modern humans, hunting down defenseless animals.

"I believe in animal control but I know there are better ways to accomplish this without that sadistic macho crap!"

Matt Driscoll once again studied the tall, red haired, and very candid sergeant. He caught her eye and smiled approvingly at her remark, as Rob Carmody simply and resignedly, shook his head.

The three sergeants from the past were becoming increasingly more aware of the changes in their new environment. It seemed to them that as every few minutes passed by in their new existence, some other novel, and often troubling, changes were being revealed to them. Some of the changes seemed difficult and yet many felt like positive changes. In Lilly French's point of view, this last one was one of the positive changes.

# CHAPTER SIX

FOLLOWING THEIR "NON-FAT" LUNCH at the NCO Club, the three sergeants, along with Captain Driscoll, climbed aboard their little shuttle and drove away from the central part of the base. Their Air Service vehicle whisked effortlessly across the well maintained roads. Even though these vehicles did not make contact with the surface, the roads obviously had been maintained along with lane lines and the proper signs, in order to control traffic flow.

There now were electronic devices imbedded in all roads and highways. These were designed to make continuous electronic contact with motor vehicles that passed over their control areas. These items had double and often triple redundancy overrides to prevent accidents in the case of damage or electronic failure. Every traffic district had control-centers that had "real-time" electronic contact with these systems. Computers at these centers would immediately spot failures and switch to secondary systems. Repair crews would then be dispatched to the problem areas. Traffic accidents were practically eliminated for surface travelers in this Fourth Millennium. Old fashioned road signs still marked the routes for the edification of the passengers of these mysterious anti-gravity vehicles.

"Most of these roads have bicycle lanes that are also electronically controlled in order to keep the motor vehicles from colliding with the cyclists."

Matt Driscoll informed his charges of this as he explained the traffic controls. They had already passed numerous people riding their bikes along the outer lanes of the roads.

"Bicycle riding is more than just a sport in our society. You'll noticed that most of these bikes are equipped with folding baskets and a carry racks over their rear wheels. They have become rather utilitarian vehicles. We all have them."

"What about old people? Do they still ride bikes?"

"Most do—Sergeant Johnson. There's a popular saying out here: 'You want to be an old person, keep pedaling. You want to be an older person than that—keep on pedaling. Of course they say the same thing about walking—keep on walking.'"

The crew headed south and Rob Carmody announced to his little group that they were traveling just above the old 13th Street access road to the base. They passed a few similar sized vehicles sliding silently above the old roadway.

There no longer was a manned perimeter gate, however Rob noticed some tiny cameras and speakers on tall metal poles where the Security Police Gate had once been. As they proceeded to the southwest he noticed that the infamous Lompoc Federal Prison was no longer there. The huge prison was gone and there was no trace of its existence left behind from that distant era. Now, rolling across the fields to the west of 13th Street were what seemed to be endless rows of grape arbors.

They then passed a sign with bold letters announcing Lake Lompoc. Rob Carmody whistled and let out a loud gasp. He had lived in the town of Lompoc for years. Lompoc had been the suburban home for many of Vandenberg's employees, civilian as well as military. When he left this, "Valley of Flowers," the population had surpassed 60,000.

Shortly after this, their vehicle reached the edge of the vast lake. The lake swung westward to the Pacific Ocean. It also stretched miles to the east stopping at a high bluff located right at the base of the city whose skyline now soared into the clear air and sparkled in the bright sun of an early afternoon in April. Directly ahead of them, the passengers looked across the lake towards a range of high hills that marked the southern boundary and a former boundary of the beautiful Lompoc Valley. To the northeast rose even more of the large city that Rob had noticed during the landing of AG-1.

Matt Driscoll had the vehicle pull up at the parking area overlooking the lake. Once the parking stanchions were extended, they all dismounted and walked to the metal railing. There were numerous bicycles lined up in the bike racks located there and a number of after-lunch bike riders walked along the railing that marked the south end of the parking lot.

Driscoll pointed out towards the lake and said:

"Major Hansen will be talking about this during your briefing this afternoon. This is where the town of Lompoc existed before the great floods. This is not a true lake however…, it is primarily sea water. Fresh water does come down from the Santa Ynez River, but the fact is that this is a '*fjord'* or bay, with tides."

Rob Carmody then pointed out into the middle of the lake and said:

"Christ ! That's where I used to live, just a little over a year ago—our time. Fifteen Thirty-Seven West Oak Avenue. Right in the middle of that," remarked Rob with feeling.

Lilly put her arm over Carmody's shoulder when she heard the pain in his voice. Rob turned back towards Lilly and Norm and replied:

"Thanks… That's okay, remember, it's a *thousand* years guys. I'm certain that there are plenty more unpleasant shocks ahead."

Rob made this last remark with a brave shake of his head and a rather reserved smile. With that subtle move he now brought himself forward to the present, and all the intriguing possibilities this might offer. Only now had his essence finally followed his awareness into the *Fourth Millennium.*

* * *

Captain Matt Driscoll opened the afternoon session by inquiring if everyone had enough to eat. Once assured that they had, he then asked what they thought concerning their after lunch trips around Vandenberg. There responses were basically questions:

"What happened out there Captain? What the devil's going on?"

"That's what Major Hansen is going to discuss with you now," stated Driscoll.

Following their lunch, and just prior to this meeting, Hansen, Brice and Hulse had driven out to the coast at the northern extreme of the base where they viewed the other great fjord that flowed up the old Santa Maria River bed. This body of water now engulfed part of the old city, and was now referred to as Santa Maria Bay. The nearby coastal town of Guadalupe was gone. It had been completely inundated, along with an endless list of coastal communities, by the tsunamis and floods of the early Twenty-Second Century.

Driscoll then told the crew that they would be issued new identification cards following Hansen's briefing. He proceeded to get a rise out of them when he added:

"You'll receive your implants at this time."

"Implants!" Their response was like an off-key chorus.

"Yes, we all have identification implants set just below our left shoulder. It is, of course, a microchip containing all pertinent identification information and a few other items that will be discussed later. It's painless and is required of every individual on earth. One of the by-products of these little devices is that we have very little premeditated crime now across the entire planet. In fact, it is practically non-existent. Naturally, there are still crimes of passion. We're still a mildly passionate and creative people. Even these crimes are quickly resolved because the authorities know who everyone is, and *where* everyone is."

"*Big Brother*? offered Jan in a questioning voice.

"No question about that Major Hulse, but we have decided that this beats the alternatives. That is, as long as we are able to maintain a fairly tight control as well on our— *authorities.* We feel that we are able to do this, and we'll get into that subject during a later briefing on politics."

"What about the ACLU ?" Jan continued.

"The what?" was Driscoll's response.

"That answers that!" Jan said this with a resigned look, while facing Tom Brice.

Major Hansen now took over and changed the subject. The five space travelers all paid rapt attention to his remarks, which they were informed, would be followed by another dramatic holographic presentation.

"Trained geologists knew about these events when they pried their way back through *Geologic-Time* with their studies of earth's violent past. Global-warming didn't begin with you guys and your fossil fuels. But you sure as hell speeded it up! Thanks a lot!"

Hansen made this remark with a smile even though, as he pointed out, the results were devastating. The smile came from the fact that he knew that blaming this crew, or for that fact, any single person from that period, was rather disingenuous.

"By the time you all took off on this mission, the die was already cast. The only thing that your burning of fossil fuels did was to speed up the normal geological cycle. Still, it would require a few more decades—actually, almost a century for the great catastrophe to appear. Are any of you aware of just how much, 'above sea-level' ice existed at the poles in your year Two-Thousand?"

His little audience collectively indicated that they had no idea.

"Roughly, there *were* two point four million *cubic* kilometers of ice resting on the continent of Antarctica and the three great Artic islands of Greenland. Prior to the cooling period of the late Twenty-Second and Twenty-Third Centuries, nearly half of this ice melted and raised the sea-level by more than twenty-five feet. Although the scientists of your time predicted a rise of a foot or two by the turn of the Twenty-First Century, it was a few inches more than twenty-five feet. Their predictions were based on a straight line warming pattern and instead it jumped exponentially near the end of the Twenty-First. Further sea rise came from 'Thermal Expansion' as sea temperatures continued to rise. During that period the earth lost sixteen percent of its formerly above sea level land-mass to the oceans and seas. This, my friends, was the most heavily populated sixteen percent!"

Major Hansen studied the shocked expressions of his audience. He knew in advance that the homes where these travelers were raised had disappeared under fathoms of water. Tom Brice's home was the only exception. His parents home in mile high Aurora, Colorado wasn't under water, instead, it was under a mass of towering skyscrapers. Denver and its former suburbs now held the nations capital, and with twelve million residents, it had become the second largest city in the country. Only the eighteen million souls living in sky-high Mexico City enjoyed a larger population. Mexico City was now the largest city on the planet.

All the crew members were educated well enough to realize that these floods alone would have been disastrous for all the great low-lying cities throughout the world.

"As all of you are aware, the largest cities in the world were established well before air travel. Naturally they were cities formed for trade and that was 'Sea Trade.' A creeping inundation of a few of these cities actually began before you all left on this mission. Naturally one thinks of Venice, New Orleans, New York and even London, to name a few that were experiencing real trouble when you folks departed back in Twenty-thirteen."

"That's right!" Brice added. "The Dutch were experiencing some difficulties with their elaborate system of dykes, sea walls and sea gates."

"That's correct Colonel. Well the troubles continued, then got worse—much worse! First, you remember the warming of the Gulf of Mexico and its effect on the strength of hurricanes. We all know about 'Katrina' sending flood waters into New Orleans. By the time you left, New Orleans was untenable and abandoned. As you all are aware, just before you left their great oil port was shut down and the resulting oil shortages, on an already troubled supply line, helped drive the changes to alternate fuel sources. There's nothing like disasters for speeding along new technologies. However, this was a little late!"

"I certainly remember that the storms were becoming much more intense," interjected Norm Johnson as if he were discussing a period way back in his early life. He was, in-fact, discussing a period of time only a few months in his past. Norm Johnson's essence, as well as Rob Carmody's, had also made the transition to 3030.

As Bill Hansen picked up the remote, he said:

"Watch and see what happened to the great cities and all the low lying lands throughout the world. Some of this is documentary footage, although a large portion is computer animation."

For the next ninety-five minutes the crew of AG-1 watched in stunned silence as they witnessed the world that they knew so well, seriously damaged by mega storms, massive earthquakes, volcanoes with their accompanying land-slides, and finally, permanent floods led by monster *Tsunamis.* The litany of great sea level cities lost to the seas and oceans seemed endless. All of them were gone and their populations were totally displaced throughout the world. A staggering percentage of the worlds population was killed by the violent earthquakes, floods, and the ensuing pandemics. Many of these quakes measuring above eight, with some reaching well past nine on the Richter Scale. These actually triggered many of the tsunamis which became one of the primary causes of population reduction.

They noticed that as the Twenty-First Century closed, most of the great low lying cities were already inundated by the rise of the oceans. Their massive populations had already moved prior to the monster tsunamis. The great loss of life was because they didn't move far enough. The culprit, the narrator of the presentation concluded, was that most humans did not want to move very far from where they themselves were raised. They built their new cities near the old ones, but on higher ground. In many cases they built them where the suburbs for the original cities had been.

The "Five" listened intently as the documentary continued. The presentation showed the newly relocated cities developing. It appeared like time-lapse photography of a plant growing, even though it was actually superb computer animation. The new cities grew on the higher ground alongside their famous original sites. The images now changed to those of our giant planet slowly turning. The Artic Ice-cap receded and disappeared, and the Antarctic Ice-cap shrank rather dramatically. The presentation then showed the great geologic Tectonic Plates building up strain as the melting ice flowed towards the Equator and added enormous weight to the plates. The above sea-level ice melted into the oceans.

There had been a number of deadly tsunamis prior to the turn of the Twenty-First Century, however, the really big ones came close together on September Eighteenth, Nineteenth and Twentieth, in the terrifying year 2102. The animation illustrated clearly the plate boundaries releasing one after the other. Even the mid-continent New Madrid Fault released below the Mississippi River causing a great loss of life many miles from the nations coasts. The earthquakes involved now reached into the *tens* on the Richter Scale. These quakes triggered major volcanoes which then triggered the giant land-slides which in-turn released the largest tsunamis.

The holographic presentation then showed a computer animation of the giant tsunamis crashing into many of the worlds new *safer* giant cities.

The "Five" simultaneously jerked their heads back from the realistic scene. It was difficult for them to fully comprehend that this had actually happened. The narration continued on:

"They—the people of that period did not build most of their new cities far enough back from their coasts. Most of these were built at least one hundred feet above the recently established sea-levels. Not enough! Most of the tsunamis crashed in-land with their second and third waves reaching more than three hundred feet in height. And, as is true with tsunamis, a great deal of the water eventually pooled and remained."

At this point in the presentation, the three dimensional depiction of the seas crashing into these new cities brought the crew members out of their seats. Even Bill Hansen and Matt Driscoll flinched and stepped back from where they were standing. Despite the fact that these two instructors had seen the show before, the effect on them was still startling.

"This is when the greatest loss of life took place," continued the narration. "The population of the earth, as we entered this period, was a little more than seven billion souls. Just over four and one half billion humans survived. It was thirty-five percent of our ancestors that died during this very brief period which included the decade directly following the great earthquakes. This is referred to as the decade of disease. Much of our medical technology and anti-biotic weaponry was lost during the disasters. Newly mutated diseases were loosed practically unchecked upon the world's population.

"Our world population right now, even with the present controls on population growth, has risen to just below five billion. This is surprising for the reasons that I am about to explain. A little known fact is that in the year Eighteen-fifty there were no more than one billion humans on this planet. By Twenty-one Hundred, even with the massive loss of life from the earlier tsunamis, there were seven billion. In two and one half centuries human population had grown six hundred percent. Such growth could not have been sustained for even a few more years. There already was wide spread starvation throughout the 'Third World' nations. The disasters were awakenings for us all in many ways. We now have very strict controls on population growth. Five billion humans on this planet is the absolute limit. These limits are strictly enforced by United Nations controls which will be discussed in greater detail during subsequent briefings. These briefings will be presented live by one of your instructors."

At this point the holographic presentation ended and Major Hansen stood up in front of the shocked audience.

"It sounds like that presentation was made for us exclusively," remarked Tom Brice. "The narrator just spoke of our subsequent briefings. How, could you get something as elaborate as that made so quickly?"

"As you were told on your arrival, we've know pretty well when you would arrive Colonel," Hansen responded. "We've known this for many years, and after you started your descent, we were able to become increasingly precise concerning your arrival time. When we put on this big welcome at your arrival, it wasn't just show. We've been waiting a long time for you—welcome back! Furthermore, this rather elaborate holographic presentation is also used as part of our high school curriculum throughout the world, so we really are getting full utilization. Only the part referring to your subsequent briefings has been added for your enlightenment.

"Now, as you have just seen, the transfer of the enormous weight of melted ice from the poles to the earth's equatorial regions, put added stress on some of the Tectonic plates, hence the huge earthquakes."

"I think we got that message loud and clear," exclaimed Tom Brice.

"My God! Nearly two and a half billion were killed in two days?" Lilly asked in disbelief.

"Not all in two days Sergeant," answered Bill Hansen. "A large percentage of those died from the subsequent plagues that swept the planet. However, the immediate loss of life was staggering."

"How did they dispose of all those bodies in such a short period of time? I take it that they must have been cremated. Identification and record keeping must have been a nightmare?"

This the analytically minded space-ship commander added as they all once more pictured in their minds the horrific scenes of masses of human bodies, as well as animal carcasses, washing ashore for months following the great disasters.

"Yes Colonel, but—this is when world wide efforts to aide the survivors brought the world together. This was the moment that changed everything. As you can imagine, it took many years, actually decades, to rebuild on truly safe ground. It took decades to rebuild our basic infrastructure, and these were very hard years for the human race. But most people pulled together and even religious differences were simply set aside. Those survivors are now looked back upon as '*The Greatest Generations.*' The use of this term is not in anyway an attempt to denigrate the brave American servicemen of World War Two who were awarded the title of '*The Greatest Generation*,' in the singular, by your Tom Brokaw in his book of the same name. Furthermore, during those disasters of the Twenty-Second Century, many family trees were ended and new ones began, devoid of the sometimes questionable baggage of the past."

Tom Brice held up his hand, then asked another question concerning this subject.

"I suppose cremation has now become the accepted practice for disposing of our mortal coils?"

"That's correct Colonel, however, it is not just the accepted practice… It's the only practice allowed. Can any of you imagine just how much valuable land would have been needed to bury two and one half billion people? That may sound rather cold, but remember, we are now in a more practical world. As Driscoll here mentioned, religions had to alter some of their ancient doctrines. They had to find more flexibility in the interpretation of their scripture. They did—and here we are.

"Now, I believe that it is time for Captain Driscoll to take you all over to Pass and I.D. as well as the Clinic, for your new identification cards and your implants. Thank you all for being such a good audience."

"Very Impressive! Great presentation!" said Tom Brice, as they all stood and shook William Hansen's hand.

"Just one more question Major Hansen and I feel that it is related to this subject."

"Yes, of course—go ahead Colonel Brice."

"We in the military and our families are all covered medically. At least I believe that to still be the case?"

"Yes—that's correct Colonel."

"My questions then are: What about the civilian population? Do they purchase medical insurance? How much coverage is there? Does such coverage include dental?"

"Whoa Sir! One question at a time if you please. First, no insurance is available or needed for civilians. They have the same coverage that we in the military always enjoyed. And, yes this does cover dental."

"Then, we have reached the point of Socialized Medicine? We were very worried about the government running the medical field in our time. The Federal Government had a knack for screwing up operations which came under its control. Don't tell me that we now have government run Socialized Medicine."

"That's correct also Colonel, however it is run by medical professionals instead of bureaucrats. It is run quite efficiently and effectively, and without cost to the public. As has been mentioned, our medicines and medical practice are first rate. Furthermore, the demand for medical attention has declined to only a small percentage of what it was back in your time, which is a testament to our entire field of medical research. If it sounds like I'm proud of these accomplishments—I am."

"I don't blame you Major Hansen, we all are quite impressed. Thanks again for your presentation."

The crew of AG-1 now reflected soberly on their first two briefings. When discussing it all with each other at the coffee shop, prior to going to Pass and I. D., they were unanimous in their relief that they hadn't returned home after only a century in space. Although, it had been a very sobering dramatization, the entire crew of five were now truly entering the new millennium and increasingly content to be there.

# CHAPTER SEVEN

At Pass and I.D. the crew members filled out a number of official looking forms. The questions about their past and their family ancestries were exhaustive. They were then photographed, scanned, and blood tested. The results of their full body scan and blood tests were returned almost immediately. They only had to wait a few minutes following this and their new I.D. cards were ready. They were informed that everyone on the planet had been issued one of these amazing little cards. Adolescent children receive them when they reach twelve years of age, normally on their birthday; it had become a sort of a ritual. Passports and Visas were documents of the past along with many other identifying items. This, and the implants they were soon to receive, were all the crew members needed to travel freely from one country to the next.

Norm studied his card and remarked how precise his three dimensional image was.

"Just a little too accurate," he joked.

The cards had a number of anti-counterfeit protections, plus all the information that each individual supplied on their forms was now encoded into the plastic cards. They were also told that the plastic cards were practically indestructible, however, no one tested this pronouncement. At this time they were advised that it would be difficult to actually loose one of these cards because there were special scanners available that could easily locate them. In an extremely rare case where one could not be located, a copy would be provided locally.

Upon arriving at the nearby medical clinic they were a little startled to see a number of medics along with a couple of doctors there to welcome them. Tom Brice noticed that there were no other patients in the waiting room and the same was true in the clinic itself. It was time for the implants and a light gray uniformed staff-sergeant medic called the crew members over to his station, one at a time, according to rank. Lieutenant Colonel Brice was the first to get an implant. He noticed that after using a moist cotton swab on the area just below his left shoulder on his upper arm, there wasn't any pain at all when the tiny implant was surgically inserted. The implanted device was about half the size similar in color to a grain of rice. He was, however, a little surprised when the medic picked up another implant similar in appearance, and inserted it just below the first one.

"What's this Sergeant?" was his immediate reaction to this.

"Sorry Sir," the first was a medical implant to give your immune system the same protection we all have. The second, of course, was your coded identification monitor."

The Colonel accepted this explanation without further comment. Major Hulse was next and the rest of the crew followed in order. It all took very little time, but Tom Brice still wondered why there were so many light gray uniformed witness's to their little ceremony.

After all of the five crew members received their implants, Matt Driscoll escorted them into the office of Vandenberg's Hospital Commander. Doctor Jeremy Atwal rose from behind his desk. He wore the silver eagles of a full-colonel on his shoulder epaulets, and he welcomed the visitors into the large office offering them the folding chairs that had recently been provided.

"Did everything go all right out there? Is anyone having a reaction to the implants?"

The crew members were somewhat surprised by the question as they turned towards each other; then everyone shook their heads indicating no negative reaction.

"All right then," Doctor Atwal smiled and then turned towards a darkened corner in the large office. He then said, with a touch of formality:

"Let me introduce the Aerospace Service's Surgeon General, Lieutenant General William Vaughan."

With this, a tall distinguished officer, wearing the three stars of a lieutenant general on the epaulets of his dress blue uniform, stepped out from the shadows. The crew members quickly came to their feet, and just as quickly General Vaughan waived them back down into their chairs.

"Welcome aboard space travelers. I'm certain that this is turning into quite an adventure for you. The entire United States of America Aerospace Service, not only welcomes you, but considers you to be five of our greatest heroes.

"As you young people have been made aware, the human genome has been altered and perfected. We have now reached a point of near physical perfection. Some of this has come about naturally in the ways that Captain Driscoll and his holographic presentation described. Now, it's my turn to fill you all in on a bit more of the alterations."

The crew members settled themselves into the folding chairs as comfortably as the could. They rightfully expected this to be another interesting and informative presentation. General Vaughan had a commanding presence which was reminiscent to each of them as they viewed the famous portrait of the base's namesake, General Hoyt Vandenberg, hanging on the wall behind the handsome and distinguished looking officer. General Vaughan studied each of the astronauts closely as he began.

"As the human race came out of the disasters of the early Twenty-Second Century, the survivors finally mixed completely without much thought of racial or ethnic differences. However, they were all very much aware of the problems of negative DNA strings and the growing problem of birth defects. These problems increased rather dramatically during the harsh survival conditions that lasted into the middle of that century.

"Then, with their new safer cities, advances in their educational system, and further breakthroughs in their scientific knowledge, they found that they could control and eventually cancel out these defects. This was also due to the fact that most of the human scientific knowledge was preserved throughout the Internet and on 'hard-drives' world wide. Most of the knowledge and data lost from the labs, libraries and hospitals in the destroyed sea-side cities was saved in our personal computers. This was in sharp contrast to the great loss of knowledge we believe was lost to the human race back in Cleopatra's time with the burning of the famous library at Alexandria, Egypt.

"By the middle of the Twenty-Third Century our ancestors could control the human genome, prevent defects and forever alter the once negative effects of regressive DNA. 'Nano Technology' had finally been perfected and we were able to work medically beneath the cellular level, even down to the atomic level."

Lilly French raised her hand at that moment. General Vaughan, expecting the inevitable question, said:

"Go ahead with your question Sergeant French. I've expected it."

"Sir! You're not telling us that they started aborting fetus's that indicated tendencies towards birth defects—are you Sir?"

"Yes Sergeant—that's exactly what they did. In fact that practice began before you folks left on this mission. The only difference is, by the Twenty-Third Century it had become mandatory, and it was enforced. They aborted these fetus's before the final period of brain formation. When the early signs of defective development indicated any of a number of known birth defects, the fetus's were aborted. Medical officers complied on threat of loosing their licenses and their practices. It had, by that time, become accepted science that the "soul" or human awareness, did not transfer from the spiritual state into the physical state until the unborn infant's brain was nearly fully formed. They were able to come to this conclusion by studying brain wave activity while the fetus was forming in the womb."

All the crew member's hands shot up on hearing this. General Vaughan waived them down while asking for a few more minutes.

"I know what your going to ask, and no, this procedure has no harmful side effects for the mother. Now, please let me finish and then I'll take your questions.

"All third trimester abortions were outlawed by that time. Second trimester abortions were allowed only on special case-by-case health demands. The necessary information to abort was normally available during the third month of pregnancy. All expectant mothers are screened during this time and informed whether or not their pregnancy would proceed. We now have the capability of studying a single cell from the early fetus and determine any and all potential birth defects that would occur. The abortions take place immediately at that time, if they are required. If a married couple has exceeded their limit, this is also a grounds for termination of the fetus."

"Exceeded their limit! Is this still the case?" A rather upset Lilly French responded.

"There is little need for abortions today Sergeant—except in the rare case of accidental injuries that might require such. But, yes—every young couple is given a limit on how many children they may have. It varies, but basically it is two children per couple. When a married couple decides not to have any children, another couple my be allowed to have three. Three is the maximum and those couples that have indicated they wanted an additional child are chosen according to the quality and compatibility of their genomes. Now, please let me continue, if you will Sergeant."

"Sorry Sir."

"Don't be sorry Sergeant. That was a natural question and I realize that this is a rather emotional topic for you all.

"The leadership of that period," continued the general, "made, what seemed at the time to be, a rather Draconian decision that they would go much further in refining the human genome. It had become normal practice by the Twenty-Second Century to demand chemical castration of convicted pedophiles. Instead of housing these individuals at considerable cost, they were returned to society with a much lowered sexual urge. A second conviction would bring 'Neuro Reprogramming.' These cases, however, were rare. Such a problem doesn't exist today, thanks to the altering of the human genome."

Matt Driscoll, sitting to one side, studied the reaction of the crew members as General Vaughan brought them up to date and into the new world of medical realities. He noticed the varied expressions of shock and dismay. He then thought to himself: *Wait until they hear the clincher.*

"Following this," the general continued:

"The next logical step in the thought process of the now unified world leadership, was to use *sterilization* to control the infusion of retarded and or seriously physically handicapped individuals. These leaders were all fully aware that such laws would be viewed as a throwback to the Nazi regime of the Nineteen Thirties. Despite this, these laws were adopted worldwide. A few generations later, following strict enforcement by the medical profession, the incidents of birth defects disappeared along with most other physical and mental disabilities. Today—they are non-existent!"

"You mean General, everyone now is *perfect!*" Tom Brice's response had the intended touch of sarcasm.

"No one is perfect Colonel, and probably never will be. But, we have come a long way. I believe that you all have been informed that there is practically no crime anymore. We only maintain small police forces which are necessary to assist, far more than apprehend. The armies throughout the world are tiny and really qualify as National Guard by your frames of reference. Their primary function is disaster relief and there have been only minor demands in this area for centuries. Actually, not very often since the Mini-Ice Age of the late Twenty-Second and Twenty-Third Centuries. The same is true with the Navy. It is no longer an offensive military force. It's now what you folks utilized as the Coast Guard for port controls and also for disaster relief. In fact, the Navy and Coast Guard have combined operations throughout North America and their primary mission is to keep the ports and sea lanes open year round. Only the Aerospace Service is large, and you'll be briefed later on what that entails."

Tom Brice's hand was in the air before the general finished his dissertation.

"Your question Colonel Brice?"

"Mini-Ice Age Sir? We were informed during Major Hansen's presentation that there was a 'cooling period' following the disasters of the great earthquakes and tsunamis. The term 'Mini-Ice Age' didn't come up in the presentation. How severe was it?"

"I believe that the presentation mentioned the hardships of the Twenty-second and Twenty-third Centuries," responded General Vaughan.

"Some scientists, even today, decline on calling this period a Mini-Ice Age, however, that's what it was. Once the oceans had expanded to the limits of the early Twenty-second Century, their true reflectivity kicked in. As you were informed, sixteen percent of the land mass of your time period had been covered by the highly reflective oceans and seas. This triggered the end of the global warming period with a higher percentage of the suns heat now being reflected back into space. The planet cooled down precipitously and the Mini-Ice Age ensued. The polar ice caps regained some of their previous depths. A few glaciers formed back into the mountain valleys of the North American Continent and similar places above the Artic Circle world wide. Because of the rather gradual encroachment of the ice and snow zones, the human population was able to reestablish itself once more in the more temperate regions."

"I'll bet that this exodus didn't go over to well with those who were already living in these more temperate climates," responded Tom Brice.

"That's right Colonel, yet this is when the human races found out that there had been an enormous change in their collective attitudes and behavior. The positive responses that took place during the disasters came into play once again during the period of ice encroachment which didn't climax until a few generations beyond the great tsunamis. This is why we refer to the people of that time as members of the 'Greatest Generations,' plural. The ice-fields have long since receded and our climate now is similar to what it was when you folks left Nevada. Naturally, the oceans and seas withdrew during the cold period and they also have returned to near the level that they were when you departed. As you have seen, there are many new lakes and bays that have remained such as Lake Lompoc and Santa Maria and Los Angeles Bays, to name a few."

General Vaughan moved across the office and pointed to a large map of the world that was attached to the wall. He then turned back to his little audience and continued:

"Major Hansen undoubtedly touched on the speed of these climatic changes, but I feel compelled to repeat this. Throughout the centuries of geologic studies scientists have referred to 'Geologic Time' in order to explain these great changes in our planet. The changes were spread over tens of thousands of years when discussing climate changes and hundreds of millions of years when referring to tectonic plate movement. Human activity has unwillingly speeded up these changes by still unknown factors. The Mini Ice Age of which I speak only lasted for a little more than one and one half brief centuries. Right now there is a subtle yet real worry concerning what will come next. As you all have been informed, we no longer flood our delicate atmosphere with carbon based emissions, so *maybe* the changes will once more slow down and we will be able to enjoy once again a stable planet. All in all, our present situation is fine and the *immediate* future looks secure when it comes to weather and human development. I must admit, however, that there are a few potential trouble spots gaining our attention. One is the recent activity in the massive caldera beneath Yellowstone National Park."

"Well Sir, aside from that, the situation right now sounds rather idealistic," responded Sergeant Carmody, after being recognized by General Vaughan.

"No wars and very few natural disasters since that Mini Ice Age period. It all sounds a little too good to be true."

"It may be Sergeant" continued the general.

"It's been nearly thirty generations since that period of disasters and since the controls I mentioned, were initiated. There were some inferior genetic lines that came through those initial decades, however, none have been detected for the last few centuries."

The five crew members reacted to this statement in unison as Matt Driscoll eyed each of them carefully.

*The moment of truth*, he reasoned.

Tom Brice spoke out the question that was on all of his crew members minds:

"You mean, no inferior genetic lines have shown up until *we* came along. Is that not so General?"

"Yes, that's quite perceptive of you Colonel."

The others gasped as a variety of unpleasant possibilities raced through their minds.

"Are we to be sterilized…?"

Norm Johnson's question hung, almost visually, in the stilled office.

"You already have been Sergeant Johnson. All of you have been sterilized. That was part of the medical procedure when you just now received your implants."

"What General—! Without our permission!"

Tom Brice was the first, but not the last to reflect his dismay.

"The first implant that you all received," continued the general calmly, "was the one that caused sterilization. The medic didn't mislead you when he said that this implant would also improve your immune systems. This was true, and the reason that there were all those other uniformed witness's was to insure compliance for the 'Leadership.' Sorry folks… It's the law. We cannot allow new, or arguably old, genetic strings to complicate our present human genome. Now, that's the way it is and it's irreversible. There should be no physical side effects, no loss of sexual drive. Unfortunately, there may be some psychological downside, and for this I apologize."

Lilly French and the rest of the crew were a little surprised at their own rather tepid reaction to the news that they had all just been reprogrammed without their permission. They all had a rather disturbing desire to be compliant and accept the fact that they had been taken advantage of. These were passionate, creative and very independent people. Yet, they all had only a rather mild reaction to the news that they would be the last of their families lineage.

"Maybe we really are inferior…"

Senior Master Sergeant Rob Carmody voiced this thought with a certain amount of conviction.

"Not inferior Sergeant—just different. When you all leave the base and travel into the nearby city of Santa Maria, you will see the benefits of these laws."

"Santa Maria," responded Rob. "I'm surprised that they've retained the name. I thought part of it was now a lake."

"That's right Sergeant," replied the Surgeon General.

"Only the northern part of the old city is now a bay, but this new city, of three million, is still named Santa Maria, the capital of California. The state is still California, and the country is still the United Sates of America. No more Mexico, Just good old USA. The United States of America, when you left had fifty states. As I believe you've been informed, we now have seventy-one. Are there any more questions?"

Janet Hulse hand went up.

"Yes Major?"

"What about 'smoking' General? I haven't seen anyone around here smoking. Is smoking banned?"

"Smoking? I've read about this. I believe it was mentioned in Second Millennium History. People actually puffed on burning tobacco leaves. That went out along with harmful drug usage just a few decades after you all left on this voyage. No—people don't *smoke* as you put it. If they did, I believe everyone would run from them as from a wild lunatic. Are there any further questions?"

Rob Carmody now raised his hand:

"What about homosexuality General. Was that also a victim of manipulation of the human genome?"

"Very important question Sergeant. The manipulation of the genome in this area, was discussed, debated, publicized and agonized over. The Church's condemnation of the practice was becoming diffused, even in your time. However, we have been aware for a long time that homosexuality was normally not the result of an individuals psychological choice; it was genetic and we realized that we could eliminate it from the human genome. Then came the big question.

"The general public was well aware of the fact that most homosexual individuals were artistically gifted. Here is where the debate began to reach a climax. Could our scientists separate the portion of the human genome that included artistic genius, from the portion that caused homosexual reactions? The answer was no; the two were inseparable. Should we head into the future devoid of a large portion of our artistic potential? What was the thing that truly separated us from lower forms of life? It wasn't the ability to make tools—even crows can do that. Creative art is the answer. Certainly, there are a great mass of creative artists that are not homosexual, however, could we afford to loose the talents of this truly creative community? The percentage of artistic genius among this group is abnormally high. Should we do without this immense source of art, music, dance, theater, and literature for some archaic homophobic reason? The answer was no, and that should answer your question Sergeant. Homosexuality is accepted in our present society and without the negative stigma of the past."

"That certainly sounds like the right decision and I feel that my entire crew agrees. We've had discussions about this sort of thing, while sitting around that large high table in our little AG-One spaceship."

"Well I'm glad you all approve of our actions Sergeant, now let me get into one other area that I want to discuss with you people. This is the area of psychological changes. I realize that Doctor Kozak gave you all a cursory psychological check, but that isn't getting into the psychology of today.

"When you folks left on this trip, the idea of self-healing had not fully taken control in the field of medicine. All of you are probably aware of endorphins and their effect on human health. I have read some of the literature on this subject, from your time. Doctor Deepak Chopra's work seems to come closest to where we are now. He felt that Medicine was an important part of human health, but this had to be combined with positive thinking to gain the full medical benefits available to each and everyone of us. We have now found that self-healing through the use and self-release of our endorphins is a major part of this field of medicine. We now know that our individual immune systems are controlled by our minds. Man becomes what he thinks about, so you'll be surrounded in this modern world by positive thinkers. It may seem strange to you all that practically everyone here seems to be happy or at least in a good mood. This is not an act—it's the way we are. Think positively about yourself. The 'Last Frontier,' your mind, has now become the 'Final Frontier.'"

* * *

That evening, Tom Brice and Janet Hulse met in the small cocktail lounge which was located in the basement of Base Operations. Tom considered it to be a stretch for alcoholic beverages to be served in this particular building. *After all--it was **flight** Operations.* Air crew members were still under a very strict code of behavior, which included no consumption of alcohol within 12 hours of flying. When he questioned Bill, the bartender, about this, he was told about another use for the implants that they had received that afternoon. It seems that they would indicate a problem when scanned if an individual was impaired by the use of drugs or alcohol. Prior to every mission, all air crew members were automatically scanned when they passed through the Fight Operations entrance and out onto the parking tarmac of the airfield. Tom found that alcohol was the one 'non-prescribed drug,' the use of which was still allowed. The altering of the human genome had greatly reduced obsessive behavior, therefore blatant drunkenness was almost unheard of in General Vaughan and Bill the bartender's new world of genetic control.

Although she was inspired by General Vaughan's positive remarks on human psychology, Janet was still quite upset about what the general had said concerning their unwelcome sterilization. She and Tom were comfortably seated in a dimly lit corner booth. The lounge was practically vacant, just one other couple some distance away. Tom had carried their drinks over from the bar; there was no cocktail waitress on duty. The music was soft, pleasant and unrecognizable to the young couple.

"It really pisses me off Tom… We should have had a choice. Christ—I really wanted to have children. It goes deep. I'm really hurt."

With this, Janet eyes became moist and a few tears slid slowly down her attractive face. Tom took out his handkerchief and tenderly wiped her cheeks. Janet pulled herself closer to Tom and grasped his hand in hers. She then squeezed it forcefully and looked up into his strong face. She stared into his large blue eyes and softly said:

"I mean… I really wanted to have your children Tom. It seems that I'm very much in love with you."

Tom jerked himself back, then studied Janet's magnificent upturned face.

"Thank God! I was worried that this feeling might be—one way. You know I'm in love with you, don't you? You've know this for some time—right?"

"Yes Tom, I know."

Tom pulled the beautiful woman even closer and kissed her deeply on her mouth. She responded passionately; the passion was still there despite the implants. At that precise moment, they both felt that their individual destinies had become sealed.

# CHAPTER EIGHT

"HAVE THEY FINALLY SOLVED the problems they had with 'Hydrogen Fuel-Cells?'"

Rob Carmody as the Crew Chief and Flight Engineer on their mission, was the most knowledgeable of the five astronauts when it came to engineering problems. He posed this question to Matt Driscoll as the crew was being driven to the Base Exchange aboard another driverless bus. It was Saturday morning the Eighteenth of April, and they had no formal briefings to attend. They all needed to purchase some civilian clothing in order to augment the limited items that they were able to carry in their light luggage.

Driscoll replied: "I believe that those problems were solved shortly after you left on this mission, Sergeant. Anyway, hydrogen fuel-cells provide the fuel to power just about every unconnected moving thing on the surface, and have for a very long time. Most of our stationary power comes from solar or nuclear energy, now that we have a use for the waste that nuclear energy creates. We'll be discussing this with you during our science briefing."

"Just a moment Captain," replied Rob. "You said 'unconnected' in discussing surface travel."

"That's correct Sergeant. Subways, surface trains and elevated trains as well, all use 'Mag-Lev' propulsion systems. Air and space-craft, of course, are powered with Anti-matter. I believe that this was already explained to you. Your mission was the lead on this technology. By the way folks, you may have already noticed that there no longer exists private ownership of motor vehicles... No more D M V! All powered transportation is public—trains, planes or busses!"

"You people must be kidding about this one... You must be joking?"

Tom stated this as he and the other's studied the young officer for a smile, or at least a hint of a smile. There was only a serious expression on the face of their guide as he continued to enlighten them on the realities of the Thirty-first Century.

"What about motorcycles? What about private ownership of light airplanes? What about boats Captain? What about power boats and yachts? Don't tell me that there aren't anymore yachts. That would take away one of my goals in life."

"Sorry Colonel... I take it that private ownership of motor vehicles was a big issue in your time. Yes, of course, I know it was," replied Matt Driscoll.

"Those old motion pictures... It seems as if everyone back then had their own motor vehicle. From what I've learned in my studies, the situation of private ownership of transportation got a little out of control. Sorry folks—no more. When it comes to boats, there is private ownership, but these vehicles are powered either by paddles, oars, or sails. Some of the larger sailing boats are still referred to as yachts, Colonel, however they are much smaller than in your day. Also, they don't have auxiliary power aboard—they're strictly sailing boats. Maybe your dream can continue, however there are rather strict limitations on their size. Thirty feet overall length Colonel, not including a bowsprit, of course. Remember... no ostentation."

"Well, at least we won't have the expense of buying a vehicle," responded Norm as the others just shook their heads or rolled their eyes over this new revelation.

* * *

Shopping in the massive base exchange was a bit of a treat for the travelers. When it came to clothing, Driscoll tried to keep them informed concerning the new *wonder* materials; there still were cotton garments, but all of these were blends. Most of the clothes were close to, yet not quite form fitting, which was predictable with everyone being tall and trim. Along with there being no obesity problem, Driscoll explained that eating disorders, such as Anorexia and Bulimia, had also disappeared with the perfecting of the human genome. Although these were primarily mental disorders, the *codes* had been discovered for actual curing of most obsessive disorders. He then briefly mentioned the metabolism pills which had become another important and safe control of weight gain. The crew members found that the variety of sizes in the BX was very limited, yet there was a fairly wide variety in styles and colors.

"I certainly hope that there is a tailor on the premises?"

Colonel Brice held up a sleek pair of dark brown trousers when he said this.

"There's nothing in my size in this store—all too long. I'm sure that will be the same problem for the rest of you, except for you Lilly."

"Absolutely Colonel," replied Driscoll, in response to Brice's question. He pointed to the back of the store and said: "There's a tailor shop right over there."

"Where are the neckties Captain?" In asking this, Norm Johnson had noticed that even those individuals in class A uniforms simply had snapped closed their rather high collars on their jackets. These were reminiscent of the World War Two uniform collars of the German officer corps, that Norm had witnessed in so many epic war movies of his time.

"No neckties Sergeant."

"I know—no neckties in the military. No neckties among civilians. No neckties world-wide— Right Sir?"

"You've got it Sergeant," said Driscoll with a broad smile.

"Shoes… Where are the dress shoes?" It was Janet's turn now.

"All the ladies shoes look like gym shoes or tennis shoes. Some of them look like small men's shoes. I can understand this while in uniform, but where are the stylish shoes? Where are the high heels, Captain?"

"You'll find some at the specialty shops Major. However, women rarely wear high heeled shoes nowadays. They went out with skirts, along time ago. In fact I believe that skirts were on their way out back in your time. Some women still have formal long dresses with which they wear high heeled shoes, though this is only for rather rare special gatherings. Sorry Major, this is how it is. Sadly, I might add—I would like to see women in skirts, like in the old movies."

Matt Driscoll made this last statement with a touch of regret in his voice.

The "Five" used their newly acquired debit cards to pay for the items they purchased, and with Captain Driscoll's help, they were able to find most of the items they needed. Following this, it was off to Uniform Sales to purchase new Aerospace Service uniforms. They all needed the new Class A uniforms as well as the less formal everyday open-collar Class B outfits. Their 'nomax' flight suits and nylon flight jackets would not have to be replaced. These items had changed only slightly during the intervening years. The items purchased at Uniform Sales, were paid for with a special card that Driscoll pulled dramatically from his wallet.

"The government pays for this. Consider this as your initial draw against your 'Uniform Allowance.' Monday we'll get your pay straightened out and your debit cards will be infused with a little more power. Actually, quite a bit more, for I've been informed that you will all be given six months pay credits at your new military grades."

"All right!" said Rob Carmody. "Sounds much better than the six days you joked about earlier—no matter how much money that is. Don't tell me Captain. I'm still having trouble getting used to the buying power difference between 'Megas' and our old dollars. I now understand that a single Mega is actually one million of our old dollars—but its present worth against today's goods and services, I'm still trying to figure out."

"Me too," added Norm, as the others agreed. "The BX gave us a pretty good reference, but I'm sure there is much more to understand."

Driscoll held up his hand, and then tried to give the "Five" a point of reference that would help in pegging the value of a Mega.

"One pair of sox for a mega, five megas for lunch, ten for dinner. One for a bus ride in town, or a ride on the subway. One hundred for a man's suit or a hundred and fifty for a woman's outfit. Rent a room for five hundred per month and an apartment for a thousand, 'Life-Lease' a 'level-one' condo for one hundred and fifty thousand. As you all have noticed, we use the decimal system for fractions of a mega. Instead of pennies, nickels and dimes, our registers just record the fraction of a mega against your debit card.

"Look here Norm—that shirt cost you three point seven megas." continued their informative guide while studying Sergeant Johnson's receipt.

"Level One condo!" interjected Lilly French. "What's that and what's a '*Life Lease*?"

"Later on I'll show you folks the three levels of condominium living that are available for lease and then we can get into 'Life-Leases' in a little more detail. Actually, I think you all will find this quite interesting."

"Sounds a little ominous to me," remarked Lilly.

"I believe it was one mega for a beer at the club," chimed in Carmody. "I'm getting hungry and I feel that it's time for lunch. What do you all say?"

"Let's go," said Driscoll. "I'm sure we can all get into the NCO club without a problem. We can just leave your purchases in the bus. No crime—remember?"

* * *

During lunch Lilly sensed something about Janet's mood that was subtle and undetected by the others. It was some sort of womanly intuition, and she was sure that the situation between Janet and Tom had changed. It was simply a subtle change in their tone and inflection when they spoke to each other. Lilly managed to get Janet alone in the ladies room, following their lunch. She approached her cautiously, saying:

"What's going on with you two Jan. It looks to me as if you two may have gotten something resolved after all—right?"

Janet Hulse looked at Lilly and said: "Christ! Does it show that much?"

"To me it does. I doubt if anyone else has picked up on it yet."

"Well—you're right Lilly. We're in love. There's no question about it now. It started in that little cocktail lounge over there at Operations. It was consummated last night in his room."

"Wow! You didn't have to tell me that. But, I'm glad you did. So when you tell me you're in love, you aren't kidding. We all expected this to happen, so when are you going to let the cat out?"

"We'll probably let everyone know before we all go into Santa Maria tomorrow." Janet said this with a sheepish grin and added: "We're engaged!"

Lilly immediately reached over and gave her friend a big congratulatory hug. They were not Master Sergeant French and Major Hulse at this moment, just good friends sharing an important moment.

After attending Sunday church services at the non-sectarian base chapel, they all headed for the city of Santa Maria in another little blue driverless bus. They were accompanied by Matt Driscoll, who had become their invaluable companion. Matt was single and seemingly unattached. He was now spending his off duty time with the famous five as well as controlling their briefings. Tom Brice wasn't sure if his assignment called for this much attention or if it was something, or someone else.

While they were heading east on Vandenberg's California Boulevard, which ran along the long avenue of state flags, Tom stood up and faced Matt and the rest of his crew, who were sitting and chatting in front of him.

"I have a little announcement to make before I turn this trip over to Captain Driscoll. On Friday evening I got up the nerve to ask our Janet here to marry me, and—low and behold, she said yes!"

His fellow crew members, along with Driscoll, stood up and cheered.

"It's about time Boss," put in Rob Carmody. "We all figured this one out about one thousand and seventeen years ago."

This got a big laugh, and then the questions came:

"When's the wedding? Are we invited? Whose going to be the Best Man?"

"Hold on you guys! All of that will be decided soon enough."

Everyone was in a happy mood when they passed through the main gate and headed east on old Route One towards new Santa Maria. As the bus cleared the final pass through the low rolling hills, Sergeant Carmody came to his feet and stared out of the large windshield. Spread across the foothills, where the Firestone Vineyards had been, were the glass and steel buildings of Santa Maria. It seemed to be a great reflective wall, of between thirty and forty story tall buildings, reaching into the clear coastal air of California's Central Coast. The bus then carried Captain Driscoll and the AG-1 crew into the heart of the great city. Their bus passed many bicycle riders heading in both directions. They noticed that none of these individuals seemed to be pedaling hard, even those climbing the long hill towards the main gate of the base seemed to glide up the steep incline with little effort. They also noticed that none of these riders seemed too worried about colliding with their driverless bus nor any of the other rather sparse number of motor vehicles heading in either direction.

The inevitable question proposed by Norm Johnson concerned whether or not these bicycles had some hidden power drive system.

"No Sergeant, they are very efficient bicycles and the riders are in fine physical condition."

"I would say they are!—" was the immediate response.

Matt Driscoll then offered: "Because there no longer is any private ownership of motor vehicles, you'll see a lot more people walking and using bicycles. It is understandable that people still want their own conveyances, especially for short localized trips. Public transportation is cheap, safe and comfortable, but the citizens still want the immediacy of their own wheels. Now, battery powered chairs are still available for the infirm. While on the subject of batteries, during my research on the electrical equipment of your time, I was surprised at how limited your batteries were. Our batteries, of corresponding sizes, are more powerful and hold charges much longer than in your time."

"Well, I should hope so," responded Tom Brice. "You all have had quite a while to perfect them."

"True Tom, but ours are more efficient by a factor of fifty," answered Matt with obvious pride.

* * *

At the center of the city was a magnificent 320 acre park filled with Liquid Amber, and tall Monterey Pine trees. Colorful gardens along with intermittently dispersed Jacaranda and Mimosa trees surrounded a picturesque lake which clearly reflected images of those trees and the stately tall buildings beyond the trees and the paths. The green and purple blooms spilling from these neatly trimmed trees reminded Lilly of the Paul Cézanne painting of a Parisian park. Lilly was also a little surprised at the advanced state of the blooms for early spring but she decided to keep any questions about this to herself at this time.

As they pulled into a parking area overlooking the small lake, Lilly French was reminded of New York City's even larger Central Park, which she sadly remembered no longer existed. She felt the loss of the old city, here, much more than during Major Hansen's briefing. Although her home town of Sag Harbor was 110 miles east of what had been the world's most renowned city, it was still *the city* to those who had lived on the eastern end of Long Island. Then her thoughts turned to her little old pre-revolutionary home town of Sag Harbor. It was gone and she was slowly coming to an acceptance of that sad fact.

"This is it folks… This is Santa Maria—our State Capital. The shops are on your left and the restaurants and hotels are on the right. You'll find a children's playground and a number of theaters at the far end of the park. There are benches and tables along the path that surrounds the lake. It's a little early for lunch so you all might walk around the lake for awhile and try to get the feel for what's going on in this new world. You'll probably have some of the locals come up to you and ask you questions. There has been quite a lot of coverage in the media about you, and I must tell you that you all are recognizable. Your pictures have been all over the news channels since you arrived."

Matt Driscoll made this announcement prior to opening the passenger door. He then added:

"The bus will remain here until sixteen hundred hours this afternoon. If you miss it, well, a cab is about ten megas, and that's only to the front gate of the base."

Tom Brice and his fiancé Janet Hulse left first and headed down the broad flower lined path towards the shimmering lake. They were followed by Rob Carmody and Norm Johnson who decided to give the couple some space. Matt Driscoll closely followed Lilly French off the bus, and she waived him up to join her while they headed for the beautiful lake which was speckled with striped ducks and honking geese.

It was late Sunday morning and the first thing they all noticed was that the paths around the lake were nearly filled with neat, well dressed people out for a leisurely walk. There weren't any people with spiked oddly colored hair, nose rings or other unpleasant looking examples of body piercing. Not even any tattoos or strange body art could be seen among the citizenry. All the women were wearing slacks and the crew members noticed also that there was no clicking of tiny heels against the curing stone walkways. To the crew from the past, it seemed like they themselves were holiday vacationers enjoying an idyllic setting. However, it wasn't just Lilly; they all felt the loss of all their relatives and their great cities of the past. It was here in this beautiful surrounding, that the tragedy of global warming became most apparent to all of them.

Things seemed almost too idyllic, almost scripted or programmed, as the visitors from another time walked slowly down the path. Lilly, often suspicious concerning appearances, wondered if the whole thing was some sort of elaborate production, staged for their questioning eyes.

"All these people cannot be walking around here, smiling, well dressed, polite in their responses to each other. It's too pat!… I don't like it. It's the Stepford Wives!"

Matt Driscoll listened to her little mumbled tirade and said:

"Stepford what?"

"Stepford Wives!…" Lilly exclaimed as she turned toward Matt then continued:

"It was a Twentieth Century motion picture in which the men of a small New England town altered or actually got rid of their dowdy and nagging wives. They then replaced them with beautiful and compliant robotic substitutions. Look at these people Captain—they seem unreal. There are hundreds of them out here and yet they're all behaving as if they're on stage. Where are the kids? Where are the pets?"

"There over there in that playground area… Look, over there to your right. See the kids on the swings and there are a number of pets on leashes over there. By the way Lilly, don't call me Captain—not when were alone… It's Matt. Actually, if you want to be formal, I should be calling you Sergeant. Although, technically a Captain out-ranks a Master Sergeant, we all know that in most cases, experience trumps rank. In fact, in almost every way, you out-rank me. Let's just be Lilly and Matt from now on—okay?"

"That's fine with me Matt, but what kind of *experience* are you referring to, and what about my question about this setting and all these people? It's all too perfect. I hear bells going off—alarm bells."

"Lilly, it's no act. In fact I don't quite understand your unease. This all seems normal to me. Remember what General Vaughan said about this during his briefing. Remember—he alerted you folks that you would notice this kind of behavior. It's an attitude thing Lilly. It has to do with how people look at things, and at life in general. Also my dear, I meant experience in a military job related context."

At this moment a small contingent of the local population came over to Lilly and Matt.

"Excuse us," said the tall smiling young man who led the little group.

"Your Master Sergeant French of the *Time Travelers,* isn't that so?"

"Yes I am Sir. I guess we can be referred to as 'Time Travelers'."

"I'm Juan Gonzales, Miss French, and I wonder if it would be too much of an inconvenience for you to sign this card?"

With this remark, the others in Juan's group produced similar cards and small pens, then politely requested autographs. Matt Driscoll held up his hand but Lilly told him that it was alright. She had never been asked for her autograph before and she found it to be strangely flattering. She also noticed that the rest of the crew were also surrounded by autograph hunters.

Matt let it go on for a few minutes, but then rather authoritatively brought the growing spectacle to a halt. He went forward to the other's, thanked the autograph seekers, then informed them that it was over.

"That's enough folks!... Thank you all but that's enough!"

What Lilly also found to be puzzling, was the immediate compliance of the gathering crowds. The people stepped back, but remained nearby, carefully studying them and the other nearby crew members, while the cards and pens disappeared back into their pockets.

She wondered why this obviously distinguished looking group of citizens would react in this manner to the request of a young military officer. These individuals weren't in the military, at least, she surmised, that they weren't in uniform and therefore on duty even if they were service personnel. Back in her time they would have paid little attention to the officer's request, yet here they obeyed like a bunch of recruits in Basic Training.

Matt knew that something like this would happen when he brought them to the park, but he also was aware that he had to introduce them to their new world. He, and his superiors, felt that they couldn't simply keep them locked up on Vandenberg Air Service Base indefinitely. With a few more words and friendly waves, the crowds finally dispersed and left the visitors to their own devices.

Once the "Five" became a little more used to their newly acquired celebrity their infusion into this culture started to become much less stressful. They all realized that much of the public *adoration* was, in fact, simple curiosity. It still was attention and that seemed to be preferable to all of them, over indifference, or possibly even avoidance.

While circling the lake, Norm turned to Rob and pointed to a nearby Liquid Amber tree.

"Rob—what's going on here? You were stationed here. Why are the leaves on these trees turning to their Fall colors? We were told that this is Mid-April. They should just be budding out... Shouldn't they?"

"I've noticed that also Norm. I'm not sure what's going on. I'm sure that they will fill us in shortly."

"It looks pretty odd Rob. Could the seasons have switched? That would mean that the magnetic poles have reversed... Nhaa!"

* * *

They all arrived back at their bus by the 4PM deadline. The travelers were filled with stories of their little adventures, and excitedly discussed them with the group. They discussed their lunches and the quality of the food. They discussed their shopping efforts and their discussions with the *Moderns.* Now, when the five of them got together they began to refer to the people of the Fourth Millennium as the "Moderns." This was done even in the presence of Matt Driscoll. It didn't have the slightest negative connotation and Matt was well aware of this. They all liked the pleasant captain and by this time they considered him as one of their own. Matt was also well aware of this, and he felt lucky to be accepted, especially when it came to Lilly French's acceptance.

# CHAPTER NINE

AT THE MONDAY MORNING briefing the travelers continued to discuss their Sunday interaction with the citizens of Santa Maria, the "Moderns." They all came to their feet when Matt Driscoll escorted a distinguished looking elderly man to the small podium that was set up for these briefings. He was introduced to them as Doctor Henry P. Cartwright, a retired NASA scientist. He had been brought here, naturally, to give them a briefing on the scientific advances that had taken place during the past millennium. What surprised the five was what Captain Driscoll said in his introduction:

"Doctor Cartwright here, has been monitoring you folks for the past eighty one years. It's been that long since they developed the ability to track and monitor a ship in earth orbit at ninety percent Warp speed. This, of course, wasn't his only duty with NASA; he was one of their leading scientists. Doctor Cartwright is one hundred and seven years old, which is not very remarkable to us, but…?"

The reaction of the five space travelers was immediate:

"Christ! You look like your in your late sixties or early seventies," responded Rob Carmody while facing their new speaker.

"Thanks Sergeant Carmody—I think," Cartwright responded.

Rob Carmody spoke up once more:

"You mention 'monitor,' as well as 'track.' May I ask--what do you mean by 'monitor?'"

"Good question Sergeant. We were able to examine your shipboard computers and study the performance of AG-One. We were not, however able to listen in on any of your verbal communications."

"Thank God for that," replied Rob Carmody with smile.

"Sir! Would you mind telling us, do we still have Social Security?"

"Yes Sergeant Johnson, and to answer your next question. The Social Security retirement age is now eighty-five. The *Fund* is only used for this and those physically or mentally disabled, which, I might add, is a very tiny percentage of the population. Our medical devices are now sophisticated enough to determine accurately if claims for disabilities are legitimate. The problem of Social Security fraud, rather rampant in your time, is presently non-existent. There are very few people on disability at this time. Furthermore, congress persons can no longer get into the Social Security Fund for any other purposes that they might dream up in order to get themselves reelected."

"Eighty-five…" responded Janet.

"That seems to establish quite a long working life for the average citizen."

"Major Hulse—when one considers the current life expectancy of one-twenty, this still means thirty-five years of retirement. Enough! That's one of the reasons you find me standing before you at my age. Retirement at eighty-five is not mandatory. I tried retirement for six boring months… That really was enough!

"Now let's get down to what I'm here for, and yes, I feel like I know all of you rather well. First, I want to talk about nuclear power. I realize that the biggest problem that you had in your time with nuclear power, was disposal of the radioactive waste. It was only a few years after your mission began that our scientists found a couple of uses for the many tons of radioactive waste created by your nuclear plants. As you know, at that time our predecessors were trying to create Anti-matter. Your ship was powered by this elusive item and only a tiny amount was created in a massive collider. Nuclear waste is where they should have been looking, and this is where they did look shortly after you left.

"I will not bore you with the technical process of extraction that they used. It was quite involved and I might add, quite complicated involving esoteric equations and engineering devices that are obviously beyond your training. Suffice it to say, they got it right. So now we have nuclear power without waste and plentiful anti-matter to power our deep space probes, and most of our aircraft for that matter. That would still leave a lot of bulk waste, but the extraction process removes the radioactivity from the bulk which then became excellent fertilizer."

Cartwright's audience smiled at this, and then he followed with:

"That old adage that everything eventually turns into shit, is quite true in this case."

His little audience laughed spontaneously at this and the formality of the mood in the briefing room rapidly disappeared. Jan turned to her fiancé and said:

"I think were going to enjoy this briefing Tommy—oops, I mean Colonel."

They all smiled at this and then Cartwright held up his hand and said:

"Alright my young friends, let's get back to the business at hand. One of my jobs during the last few years of your flight was to try to come up with a formula that would allows us to calibrate 'time-jump' at steadily increasing speeds. Obviously, we wanted to know what the time jump ratio was at varying percentages of Warp-Speed. They were right to limit your mission to ninety percent of light speed.

"I'll use miles instead of kilometers when discussing these items with you. I was told that only Major Hulse is truly comfortable with the Metric System. In the past, well before my time, they sent two volunteer missions out to punch through that light-speed barrier. Of course, unlike your mission they were never heard from again, and we feel that they might show up in a few million years, or more realistically—never."

With this statement Lilly said:

"Whew—that was a close one!"

The other's agreed as one hundred and seven year old Henry Cartwright continued:

"As you all are well aware, the astronauts on the Space Shuttles only recorded millisecond time changes and they weren't sure if these numbers would grow in a linear boost with speed increases, or would these increases be exponential. As you all have so graphically illustrated, the answer is exponential. Now, the only problem with this was that these *exponents* seem to change as well, especially as you closed near light speed. What we had to do was find a speed, a percentage of Warp, or Light speed, that would be acceptable for future exploration. They couldn't send our space explorers out with little or no chance of ever retrieving them or their information during a normal earth bound life time."

Norm Johnson asked the question that all of them had:

"What did you scientists come up with as an acceptable *time-jump*?"

"That was the question, Sergeant Johnson. That was the burning question, and the answer was a ratio of one for three. They decided that for every hour in space the speed should not cause the loss of more than three hours on earth."

"And, that speed is?" It was Tom Brice's turn to get the pertinent question in.

"And—the answer is…"

Cartwright said this with a smile while imitating a Twenty-First Century game-show host.

"And—the answer is, one million and sixty-eight thousand kilometers per hour. Pardon me, for you individuals that are still on miles per hour—six hundred and sixty three thousand miles per hour, give or take a couple of hundred miles. This speed doesn't even reach a percentage of Warp-Speed that is usable in discussion. It means that we can visit the moons of the giant planets in our solar system, however we really are locked into our solar system for most manned missions. Visiting the moons of Jupiter, which we do frequently for reasons which will be covered in my holographic presentation, takes between four months and one year, depending naturally on which quadrant of it's orbit it is in at the time of our missions and how long we intend to remain. For our astronauts this requires between one and three year of earth time."

Henry Cartwright's holographic presentation on scientific advances then leapt from the far wall with dramatic computer enhanced imagery. The breakthroughs ranged from entertaining to startling. It brought the crew a new understanding of how vehicular traffic was controlled, inter-solar system space missions, climate control devices as well as additional information concerning nano-technology and the stunning medical advances accomplished by the doctors, engineers and scientists of the new millennium.

Following this came documentary footage of the space stations. The International Space Station of the 21st Century had long since been abandoned. With anti-gravity drive ships, it wasn't necessary.

However, the scientific communities world wide decided that we needed planet bound tracking stations as well as mining and manufacturing plants that could take advantage of low gravity, pure space vacuum and unobstructed vision. Because of this, they had developed large complex space communities on our moon and on the planet Mars. The presentation showed the three moon stations, and the one Martian station, with their myriad of geodesic domed covers which were formed from minerals found at their locations. The largest of the three on our moon was the Neal Armstrong Lunar Station located on Tranquility Maré.

It seemed to the viewers that the Armstrong Station had about a dozen very large domes. The presentation took them inside these domed villages and all were surprised at the level of sophistication and life style they afforded.

"We keep about twelve hundred permanent party at that one," said Henry Cartwright on his "voice-over" microphone.

"Most of you will be heading out there once you receive your new assignments. You'll also have the chance to go to the Martian station now that you are all rated astronauts."

This brought a positive reaction from the adventurous five.

The presentation continued, showing the smaller tracking stations, one set up for mining located at the moon's equator and the other, a rather grim looking station well over into the "dark-side."

"I hope we can avoid that last one," put in a wide eyed Sergeant Johnson.

"Actually, that's the one the gives us the best view of the universe, the Aldrin Tracking Station and Observatory at the Tsiolkovsky crater. That's the most valuable of the three, but it is a little depressing being stationed at any of these stations for three months, especially with their understandable policy of unaccompanied tours for married personnel. As all of you are aware from your orbiting beyond the moon's track, and contrary to popular belief, there's plenty of sunshine on the moon's 'dark-side.' It is, however, in an electronic blackout as far as earth contact is involved. That is why this is such a valuable position for our biggest radio telescope—no earthbound interference."

Cartwright continued:

"I pulled a tour up there at 'Buzz-Base'... It was great using those powerful telescopes with their uncompromised view, yet one tour's enough!"

Then the colorful three dimensional presentation switched to an aerial view of the giant Perez Station located near the equator of the red planet Mars. It was named for Miguel Perez, the first astronaut to set foot on Mars, back in the year 2036. The presentation went on to say that there were 34 large geodesic domes and a permanent population of 4,000 on the Martian station. Mars has more gravity than the moon, therefore the inhabitants could remain for longer periods of time without experiencing the harmful effects of low-gravity. They still had to maintain an aggressive exercise regimen like their counterparts on the moon stations. As promised, the presentation also illustrated the highly successful mining operations on some of the moons of the three giant gas planets, Jupiter, Saturn and Uranus.

Henry Cartwright then discussed the Aerospace Service's partnership with NASA. This alliance had grown perceptibly since it had been the 'Air Force' prior to the departure of AG-1. This was the main reason that the Aerospace Service had increased while the other military services had declined, in numbers of personnel. Following this informative presentation, Cartwright asked if there were any questions.

Tom Brice stood up and asked a question that they all had been wondering about:

"Doctor Cartwright, we've been wondering if there had been any further contact with the small space beings that crashed in the desert near Roswell and later near Aztec, New Mexico back in the Nineteen Forties? I guess that it's no longer a secret that our ship was designed as a result of reverse-engineering of those ships."

"We are aware of that Colonel Brice, now let me fill you in on what has taken place. As you know, there were some credible UFO sightings following the Roswell incident. Most were not; often merely hysteria, yet, some were the real thing. It seems that our visitors from outer space have become a wee bit more careful when making low earth approaches. We haven't had any uncontrolled arrivals since Roswell and Aztec, but they are there. They don't respond to our communications and they certainly don't seem to be very friendly."

"What about abductions?" Jan leaned forward in her chair and repeated:

"What about abductions Doctor Cartwright? I knew someone who was abducted and their story was quite credible"

"Correct Major Hulse. There have been many verified abductions. It seems that they are trying to refine their own 'genome.' We have, as I've stated, attempted to contact them and help them with strengthening of, what we believed to be, their steadily deteriorating genetic codes. We believe that the violent past of the human race causes them great concern, even fear. These, as you are aware, are small and rather fragile beings. Certainly they have the ability to drug and disable those that they abduct, and some of these individuals have never been returned. Because of this, we believe that they fear open contact with us. Their ships are able to go to stealth mode, even in broad daylight. We cannot capture them, and our political leadership considers these abductions as merely an unfortunate nuisance. When I say that there have been many verifiable cases since you left, they number in the dozens over that thousand year period—not hundreds or more."

"Where are they from?"

Norm Johnson was the first to voice another question that all of them wondered about.

"We still don't know Sergeant. This one bugs me and everyone else. We figure that they must have pushed their speed up to light speed and probably way beyond, although most of us have our doubts about penetrating this barrier, as I have already mentioned. We're quite certain that they didn't stay in their small ships for prolonged durations, which would be required if they traveled interstellar distances at light speed or less. We know that they are not from our solar system which has now been fully explored. Therein lies the dilemma—where the hell are these little gray guys from?"

"What about the bending of space, creating 'time warps?' Rob Carmody continued on this track: "What about creating 'worm holes?' Is that a possibility Doctor Cartwright?"

"Yes it is Sergeant. That's what we feel that they might be doing, although we're not sure. It still might be inter-dimensional travel. I believe that you are all aware of the 'M' or String-theory and its eleven dimensions? The problem is that we haven't solved either of these ourselves. Not yet!"

"What about Robots?"

Carmody now abruptly changed the subject as a mass of technical questions raced through his mind.

"What about robots Sergeant Carmody…?

"We were led to believe that as robots or 'androids' became more and more sophisticated, that they might try to take over."

"They're simply our tools Sergeant."

Cartwright's response seemed to have a slight edge to it as he continued:

"We program them and they certainly have no soul or aware essence. I fear that those stories were merely 'Science Fiction' contrivances. They still write scenarios about robot revolts. No one today in their right mind is going to spend the time and money needed to perfect a more advanced breed of robots for some nefarious purpose. However, I must admit that some who weren't exactly in their right mind—, have tried… Unsuccessfully. Robots have made it possible for most of us to work at home, at least those individuals that used to be involved with manual labor. As you have seen, our highways are not heavily traveled, and then only by public or commercial vehicles. Now—are there any further questions?"

"Doctor Cartwright" Tom Brice raised his hand for this one.

"Go ahead Colonel Brice; what's on your mind?"

"Sir—we've been informed that everyone on earth now is a combination of all the varieties of human life, all racial and ethnic differences. Everyone on earth; a little difficult to grasp or even believe."

With this statement, Tom Brice looked at Matt Driscoll, informing Cartwright of the source of this information.

"I respect you skepticism. Captain Driscoll was briefed to say this and keep his presentation simple, until we could go into more detail. Please don't be critical of the Captain. He's a nice young boy and does what he's told—don't you Mathias?"

Matt grinned at this and crossed his eyes, as everyone laughed out loud.

"Actually," Cartwright continued, there are a number of isolated groups located in Central Africa, the Jungles of Borneo and Sumatra, to name a few, that refused to assimilate. We did not force assimilation but we have spent extensive time and money trying to re-educate the holdouts. We promised them all a higher standard of living and a longer life. To some, this meant absolutely nothing. We were, however, able to extract some of the DNA from every tribal group and incorporate it into our final 'Epi-Genome.' Naturally, the DNA properties that caused the diminutive size of most of these native peoples was a chromosome rejection in the incorporation process. We did not set out to block such genes, we were looking for the optimum, and we weren't certain how it would sort out. We all could have ended up much shorter than we now are, but the dominant genes were the tall ones. We also feel that our visitors from space, or another dimension, may have finally got this genetic information and infusion through those much publicized abductions. The reason for this is that their present space ships are reported to be quite a bit larger than earlier. We've determined this from recorded observations made during those very brief instances when they have *uncloaked their ships* and we were able to study them."

"Where is Science heading now Doctor Cartwright?" came the provocative question from Lilly French:

"Now that mankind has conquered disease, poverty, space and even *ostentation*—where do we go from here?"

"Even ostentation... Very funny Sergeant French. I mean that, that's amusing. Now to answer the legitimate portion of your question.

"Space... We've just touched the surface, and your mission has certainly helped. Although the three for one time jump-limitation is in effect for most of our local exploration, we are still interested in the nearby star systems. From our observatory on the dark side of the moon, we have been able to establish that there are blue planets revolving around some of those single star systems that may be within range of future large long range star ships. A couple of these stars within a fifteen light-year radius also have the protective gas giants in orbits beyond their small blue planet, such as we enjoy. As you all are aware, our gas giants, Jupiter, Saturn and Uranus, with their powerful gravities, serve as catchers mitts for harmful loose asteroids and meteors. We couldn't have built and advanced civilization without them. Obviously the same is true throughout the universe. We feel that an advanced civilization *may* have developed on one of these nearby star systems. Is that answer to your question sufficient Lilly, I don't want to seem *verbose...*"

Doctor Cartwright said this with a wink and a quick smile as Lilly returned the smile and nodded her head.

"Another question Sir!"

Rob Carmody raised his hand and leaned forward:

"What about meteors or comets striking the earth. Have any of these events happened over the past thousand years. I mean meteors of size. I realized that meteorites come into the atmosphere hourly. Have there been any 'major-events' of this sort during the past millennium?"

"Good question Sergeant. No comets, but this is a good time to discuss 'Nudge.'"

"What was that…? Did I hear you say 'nudge?'

"Yes Sergeant, just another delightful acronym. 'N-U-D-G-E' stands for Nuclear Uniform Deflection Generator. We just add the 'E' to make the point. The point is that this device is used to nudge the incoming Near Earth Object out of its potential collision track. Now to answer your question Sergeant Carmody. Yes, we have had three such events since your departure. Two of the meteors were large, about two kilometers in diameter, while the other one, 'Apocalypse' was enormous, being nearly fifty kilometers long and twenty kilometers thick. Lucky for us the two smaller ones were heading in earlier in our technological development, and they taught us plenty."

"What sort of damage would the large one have caused if it had struck the earth?" Tom Brice's question was on the minds of all of the crew members.

"Let's put it this way Colonel—none of us would be here now discussing this if this event had been allowed to happen. If the deflector hadn't been placed on the incoming meteor and activated at the time and place that it was, all human and most animal life on this planet would have ceased. Your orbiting space ship probably would not have been affected and you would have just now landed on a nearly lifeless planet. Naturally microbes and some ocean species of life would have survived and maybe a few billion 'piss-ants.'

"Let's hear it for 'Nudge,'" chimed in Norm Johnson:

"Now, just what is 'Nudge' Doctor Cartwright?"

"Again—the mechanics of that machine are quite involved, but in layman's terms it is a nuclear driver, powered by 'anti-matter' that is used to force the meteor out of its solar-orbit that interdicts the earth's solar-orbit at the same interval that both bodies arrive at a common point. In other words, this machine is used to prevent a catastrophic collision. The earlier our scientists on Tracking Station Aldrin, or 'Buzz-Base,' can predict the collision, the smaller amount of 'nudge' is required. Buzz-

Base, as I mentioned, is the far-side moon base located in the Russian discovered area known as Tsiolkovsky Crater. The primary mission there is to track Near Earth Objects. ”

“How large is this deflection generator you call ‘Nudge’ Sir?”

“Colonel Brice… If it wasn’t for the work of your team and a few subsequent space crews, they wouldn’t have been able to lift that five hundred ton ‘Nudge’ which is what was required to shove ‘Apocalypse’ out of its track. Naturally, we used anti-grav drive and our largest space ship at that time. This event took place in twenty-seven fifty-six. We landed on the meteor thirty-seven years before it’s predicted impact with earth. This required a long series of burns to get that big rock far enough off its original track to allow us some breathing room. Meteors, asteroids and comets have a knack of changing orbits when they pass close to the sun and our calculations have to be continuously recalibrated. With ‘Apocalypse’ we allowed for a larger margin of error. Obviously, the burn time was sufficient.”

“Doctor Cartwright—what about the ‘Big Bang’ theory? Do the present day scientists still subscribe to this theory as being the beginning of our universe, the beginning of time? I noticed that there wasn’t any mention of this in the holographic presentation.”

“Sorry about that Sergeant Carmody. That theory still remains the bedrock hypothesis concerning the forming of *our* universe. However, this is no longer considered the beginning of time. It certainly must have been a rather large explosion in that we are still flying apart from it. But—now it is felt that it was just one of an endless series of such explosions that have occurred since the beginning, if in fact there was a beginning.”

“There must have been a beginning Doctor Cartwright—everything has a beginning.”

“And, everything has an end Sergeant French? If that is so, the beginning may well have been *Biblical.* However, from our giant telescopes on Buzz Base, we have recently located some galaxies that, judging by their ‘Doppler-effect,’ are moving in an independent direction. Through the use of spectrographic analysis we believe that they are part of a different universe. They seem to be part of another ‘Big Bang.’ The thirteen point seven billion year age of our universe may be only a blip in the time and space continuum.

“Now my young friends, many people respond to this by saying:

'Who cares about these enormous time-frames? I'll be long gone and my loved ones will also be long gone. We'll all be long gone...' Wrong! One's essence, one's awareness, is indestructible. Whatever form it may take, it will be somewhere. Our awareness is perpetual. All of us sitting here will always be *somewhere,* and there will be periods of time that we, or should I more accurately say, you will be fully aware of this. When an individual dies, they obviously go into a *non-conscious* state, as opposed to an unconscious state. In such a state, the passage of time is not experienced no matter how long it may be. Therefore, when your awareness or essence returns to a conscious state, there will be no sense of the passage of time. With this in mind, we must surmise that the trip from this consciousness to the next will be immediate, or *seamless.* I advise everyone to take an interest in the future, for we all will be there!"

The five travelers, along with Matt Driscoll, seemed shocked by this rather definitive pronouncement. They all reflected for some time on Cartwright's final remarks. None of them had really thought about this subject in that light. There was a subtle feeling creeping into their consciousness that this one hundred and seven year old man might just be right.

At this point, after establishing that there were no more questions, Henry Cartwright stepped down from the podium and turned the meeting back to Matt Driscoll. With this, the crew members all stood up and gave the venerable and highly informative scientist, a big hand.

Matt Driscoll moved to the podium and stated:

"Our next stop is 'Pay and Accounting,' and now you can find out just how much money you'll make in your brand new Aerospace Service. You can have your debit cards updated with six months pay credits, and I might add that following this weeks briefings you all will receive thirty days paid leave."

"Hey that sounds great—but where will we go. The cities we know are gone." Sergeant Carmody said this with a faint smile of appreciation, along with some real concern.

"We'll get into this a little more during the week," answered the captain.

"I would advise our Nation's Capital in Denver, Colorado; in fact I think that they are in the process of setting up something for you over there. The 'Mile High City' survived the disasters practically unscathed, therefore, it was a logical choice. That's your home-town, isn't that so Colonel Brice?"

Tom Brice nodded his head in affirmation.

"I believe that you'll notice a few changes when you get there…"

# CHAPTER TEN

It was Tuesday morning, the 21$^{st}$ of April, when the crew members arrived at their regular briefing room. This time the sign on the door stated:

PLANS & ASSIGNMENTS + CUSTOMS & TRADITIONS.

Lieutenant Colonel James Caldwell welcomed the "Five" along with the ever present Captain Matt Driscoll. Following Driscoll's introduction of the new briefing officer, James Caldwell began his presentation:

"As the good Captain has just informed you, I am Chief of the Personnel Office here at Vandenberg. Our office handles both civilian and military assignments, along with all phases of personnel actions, complaints and reviews. Fourteenth Aerospace Service Commander, Major General Morehouse has agreed with me in assigning you crew members to 'shuttle-duty.' She has also agreed that we should keep you together as a crew on your ship AG One."

Colonel Caldwell looked directly at the officers Tom Brice and Janet Hulse, who were sitting next to each other, as he made this announcement.

This drew a mostly positive response. The compatibility of the crew members towards one another had become obvious. The stress of the past few days had brought them closer together than ever before. The fact that a love affair had developed between the two officers was only known outside the crew by Matt. His own blossoming relation with Sergeant French had a silencing effect on his possibly offering up this information to his superiors. Colonel Caldwell was Matt Driscoll's commanding officer, and he and Matt had discussed the assignments prior to making final decisions. Matt had not been in a position to discuss these new assignments with Lilly. He watched her expression as the announcement was made. Lilly was well aware that Matt was not air-crew rated.

*Shuttle duty... Interplanetary shuttle duty. My God—we'll be separated for months on end.* Lilly's troubled expression mirrored these thoughts.

Lilly's hand shot up with a less than lady like wave.

"Yes Sergeant French?" replied Caldwell.

"Are you saying Sir, that the ship will require a photographer for interplanetary *shuttle* work?"

"I'm sorry Sergeant, I should have been more specific. I meant that we will keep the space-ship's operational crew together. This means Colonel Brice, Major Hulse and Senior Master Sergeant Carmody. You and Sergeant Johnson, on the other hand, will be assigned to Flight-Operations here at Vandenberg. If I'm correct Sergeant French, you are an A, two, three, two, seven, one, Aerial Rated Still Photographer. Is that correct?"

"Yes Sir Colonel! I'll be looking forward to this assignment." Her tense body relaxed after this explanation and she settled back in her comfortable chair.

After watching Lilly's expressions throughout this exchange, Matt also relaxed and thought to himself: *She really does care about me. My lilly would now be spending most of her time with me here at Vandenberg.*

Colonel Caldwell now continued with the briefing:

"Your ship is presently being refitted with updated electronics, including modern navigational devices and a new, more efficient, drive system. The interior is being redone as well. As a shuttle, you will be carrying eight passengers as well as you three crew members."

"Pretty small spaces, Colonel Caldwell. It's a pretty small ship for interplanetary shuttle work. It seems to me that it would be awfully cramped and uncomfortable for multi-month round-trips, at even one third earth-time travel, especially out to the moons of those gas giants. Even at more than six hundred thousand miles per hour—, it seems as if it would be impossible to carry enough supplies and provide sleeping arrangements for eleven people."

"Whoa—hold on, okay Tom… I'm sure you don't mind me calling you by your first name. Tom—we have naturally considered the problem concerning the size of your ship. The plan was never to use your ship for 'Deep-Space' missions. You three will be performing personnel shuttle service to *our* moon bases. Your ship, along with six other ships will be making this run exclusively. Three of those six shuttles are large bulk carriers. You will join the three others as personnel carriers. Your ship is the smallest and will be used for transporting senior personnel. You're typical round-trip mission will be seven days with less than eight hours confined aloft."

"Alright, thank you James, if I may call you that. You know—Colonel to Colonel and all that. You had us a little worried there for a moment. According to what you have just explained, we will have five day layovers at the moon stations. That sounds pretty good but that might become a little boring after the first few days. What do you think about this Janet, and you Rob?"

"Sounds great to me Boss—oops, I mean Colonel," answered Sergeant Carmody.

"I'll have plenty to keep me busy. As a Crew Chief, most of my work is at the airfield after we've landed."

Janet Hulse just looked at her intended and smiled approvingly. Her mind raced ahead and she wondered what making love with her man in low moon gravity would be like. She thought about this for a few seconds and simply responded with:

"Whew."

The others noticed this subtle display, understood and smiled.

"You won't be bored Tom. You and Janet will be assigned plenty of additional duties on the moon, just like all aerial rated crew members here on base, and back through history, if I'm correct."

Colonel Caldwell now went into detail concerning the various assignments and additional duties that all of the crew members would be given. After this rather exhaustive presentation the participants broke for lunch.

* * *

Following lunch at the local clubs, Colonel Caldwell continued his briefing. This time the subjects were Customs and Traditions, and not just of the Aerospace Service but those of the general population.

"In this portion of the briefing we'll watch a holographic presentation put out by the Aerospace Service, which should get you all up to speed concerning the modern customs and traditions of the service. It should fill you in on our present mission requirements. But first, I would like to discuss with you the status of religions in the modern world. I am aware of the fact that Captain Driscoll briefly discussed this subject with you. Now, I would like to go into greater depth, and I am requesting that you do ask questions so that we can get a proper understanding of this rather emotionally charged subject."

With this, Colonel Caldwell studied the now serious expressions of his audience.

"When you folks departed on this mission, the world wide status of religious belief was in turmoil, to put it mildly. It seems that we were entering World War Three at that moment, and it was definitely a religious war. It wasn't just religious differences. Class warfare once again, or more correctly, continued on to raise it's troubled head. As you all are well aware, it was the brink of *Armageddon...* It, also, was the pinnacle of illogical fanaticism. Members of the other less obsessive nations, which made up the majority of the worlds population, including Japan, India and China—watched from the sidelines, in horror, as the world headed for destruction. Only some effective limited military interventions and much brilliant diplomacy prevented the nuclear exchanges that would have undoubtedly ended human life on this planet. Much of that fury was over who was the true great deity. Who was it that we were supposed to pray to and thank for placing us onto this rather pain filled planet?"

"It wasn't us who started this thing! Those other fanatics started it long before we became involved. The problems started before the United States was even a nation!"

Janet's remarks and tone indicated her personal displeasure with the direction the conversation was headed, however it helped punctuate the very point of Colonel Caldwell's presentation.

"I hear your emotion Major, but we have come to the conclusion that placing blame is immature. Sorry dear—but that's what it is. It belongs in the school yard. The Western and Middle-Eastern religions were all guilty of brainwashing their constituents, while the religions of the Far-East seemed a little more tolerant. Let's get one thing straight. The myriad of divergent religious beliefs that were present in *your time* were the result of superstition and just plain ignorance. Not stupidity—my dear, just ignorance."

With this rather indelicate pronouncement, all five crew members were shocked, yet each felt that their own internal emotional responses were again, somewhat muted.

"Now, if you'll all bear with me, I'll explain the present situation when it comes to religion. It is now believed that all religious people will proceed to the *'After-life'* that they believe in, and that is part of their particular religion. There they will be surrounded by their own, but they will not find a 'Hell,' nor a 'Heaven." No matter how bad their behavior while in an embodied state, there will be no Hell. This then is the 'first' spiritual level after death, for our individual awareness, our essence."

"No *'Hell'* James…? What about those paranoid schizophrenics such as Adolf Hitler, Joe Stalin, and Genghis Kahn. What about such sadistic bastards as 'Vlad the Impaler.' No retribution for the millions that they slaughtered?"

"You just answered your own question Tom. I believe you just said *paranoid schizophrenics and sadists*—didn't you?"

"That's right! What about them?"

"Should a handicapped individual be condemned for his handicap? Should the mentally ill be sent to an eternity of pain for a defect that they had no control over? Should inherently stupid individuals be assigned to the fiery pits because they couldn't understand the acceptable protocols of this life?"

"Excuse me James, but should such individuals be allowed to run rampant through our society, committing crimes against humanity, without constraints?"

"The answer to both questions, mine and yours Tom, is no! The difference is that I am speaking of the 'After-Life' and you are referring to this embodied life. Of course we must control the anti-social behavior of individuals. We need police forces and we used to need armies to institute these controls. In recent centuries, the controls have to do with education and human genome alterations. But, in the 'After-Life' that I was referring to, such things aren't necessary, nor is there a 'Hell' for the handicapped. *All* anti-social behavior, we now believe, comes from mentally handicapped individuals. These handicaps may be very minor such as are endured by most of us."

With this pronouncement, Colonel Caldwell spread his arms as if to include every one present.

"Or, they may be the extremes that you mentioned Tom. This is true whatever the outward motivation may seem to be. Even the crimes of the alcohol or drug impaired originate in a mind that is somewhat compromised. Normally such an individual has a very compulsive personality."

"Most people that I know are intellectually compromised at one point or another during their lives. Isn't that so Colonel?"

"That helps reinforce my point Sergeant Johnson. 'Hell' is not waiting there for the emotionally or mentally flawed. A 'benevolent' God is not going to become so sadistic as to damn his subjects to eternal pain and terror for his own or 'evolutions' shortcomings in the development of those very same human beings."

The entire crew seemed to reflect on this exchange, and Colonel James Caldwell felt that he could see the understanding of this new reality begin to penetrate. Matt Driscoll had mentioned that he thought that this crew would be receptive to these new ideas, with a possible exception or two.

"The ancient religions felt that they needed this fear of *damnation* in order to retain a submissive flock of parishioners. These threats are no longer used, yet, as Matt here already explained, our church services are well attended.

"Now let me continue on the present concept of the 'After-Life.' I mentioned that at the first spiritual level a person reaches after the death of their physical embodiment, they will encounter a level compatible to their beliefs. This is true even for those who have no religious beliefs at all and for the Atheists as well, which are two distinctly different groups. They, at this time, will experience a form of spiritual introspection even some emotional retribution. Those who have not progressed enough in their embodied state will be returned once more to this embodied state as newly born. If the character of their essence doesn't improve to meet the standards of the 'Second Level,' they will be returned again and still again, until they get it right. Character passes through to the new-born, even though *most* memories are scrubbed during the trauma of rebirth. No one would want infinite memories from past lives and there certainly wouldn't be room in our limited embodied brains. Therefore, if some of you still think that there is a Hell—*this life* may very well be it.

"Finally, when a particular awareness reaches the point of acceptance, that awareness will move up to the Second Level of the disembodied spirit world. This level we know nothing about because no one in their 'Near-Death' experiences has penetrated this level. This *may* be the 'Heaven' that is often proclaimed, but we don't preach this either. One can only continue to speculate."

"How do you know these things?" asked Lilly French.

"How can you be certain of this…? Even in this new modern culture of yours—how can you be so damn sure?"

"We're not sure Lilly… No one who says their certain about such spiritual questions, can be taken with absolute seriousness. However, during the past few centuries we have studied 'Near-Death Experiences,' with a more scientific approach than in your time. We have used 'Hypnotic-regression,' and some other rather obscure techniques, to try and discover the truth and solve this age-old dilemma."

"That's still very subjective Colonel," responded Janet Hulse.

"'*Near-death*,' it seems to me, is well short of actual *After-Death*."

"It is somewhat subjective Janet—but it's all we have. What we found to be fascinating was a strong bond of similarities in the comparison of 'Near-Death' experiences. These similarities cross cultural, linguistic and geographic lines. These experiences are surprisingly analogous throughout the world, regardless of language and custom differences. Even centuries ago, when we reached beyond the limitations placed on individual free-thought by dogmatic religious doctrine, our ancestors were able to penetrate these 'Near-Death' experiences to their very core. We have filed hundreds of thousands of such experiences to draw our present beliefs from. We are close to *certain* concerning our present conclusions."

"So then—this is the way it is?" remarked Rob Carmody.

"This certainly is the way we believe it is Rob. Maybe in the Fifth Millennium, this will change. It is our strong belief that if there are any changes concerning the *'After-Life,'* these changes will be subtle—they will be slight. You folks, along with me, are experiencing a very long trip and I firmly believe that the *long-term* future looks promising. Remember this… We are all *victims* of our own flawed characters and personalities."

"This is an awful lot to digest James. We have gone through our lifetimes with rather specific guidelines concerning religion and ideas concerning what happens after our death. Your asking us to change these views just because you and Matt here, say so. I don't know Colonel Caldwell. You're asking a lot from us poor *ancients.*"

"Tom—you say you've gone through life with rather specific guidelines concerning what happens next, right?"

"That's correct James."

"Please, I would like each of you to answer for me the following question. What's your religion? Starting with you Tom."

"I'm an Episcopalian James, but you should already be aware of this seeing how much information you seem to have on all of us."

"That's right Tom, but now I'll make my point for all of us."

"You Janet—what's your faith?"

"I'm Lutheran, German ancestry you know."

"Now you Rob, Irish Catholic. Correct?"

"Yes Sir—Irish Catholic ancestry from County Kerry in the old country."

"Baptist? Is that correct Norm?"

"Yes Sir—and a true believer, at least until now. Now I'm not so sure."

"Lilly, what's your religion? There wasn't anything listed in your file."

"That's correct Colonel Caldwell. I do believe in the spiritual world but not in any particular religion. I feel their influence is correct when they teach us to help our fellow man, or woman, whatever. I feel that their influence is incorrect when they teach that they are the only true religion, often condemning all others to Hell. I guess that makes me an Agnostic."

"Now I come to my point Tom and the rest of you. Here we have five people, all of which have different ideas concerning the 'After-life.' It's a veritable hodgepodge of divergent beliefs. Four of you are Christians, yet members of different sects. Often these sects are fiercely divided by the varying interpretations of biblical passages that we all are aware are ambiguous at their best. As I already mentioned, there is room for all of your divergent beliefs among us 'moderns.' Also there is a large percentage of people like you Lilly, that have no particular church but still believe in the spiritual world and an awareness beyond this experience, which pretty much has become the accepted philosophy of today."

With this remark, Matt smiled at Lilly as if to say that he agreed with her position. Lilly caught the glance and understood.

"If I was discussing this subject with a hundred individuals from your time, could you imagine how many divergent religious beliefs would be identified. What about thousands of individuals from nations spread out across this planet? How many different religious sects would have been identified if we had questioned thousands of people throughout the world at the time you all departed? To reach a point of workable interaction between the peoples of this planet a compromise had to be reached. This meant the modifications of the extremes of all these religions."

Without exception, the crew members seemed to understand Colonel Caldwell's dramatic point. They even seemed open to accepting this new logic when it came to each of their individual religious beliefs. Colonel Caldwell continued his discussion with his intensely interested little audience.

"It also meant the coming together of the divergent factions of these great religions. We no longer have the inter-faith designations of Catholic, Episcopalian, Baptist, Lutheran or any other of the myriad breakouts of the Christian Religion. These individuals are all Christians… That's it! We no longer have the long time warring factions of the Muslim Religion. They are simply Muslims. The same is true with the Jewish Religion, The Buddhists, the Hindus and every other religion. This kind of inter-faith fracturing was detrimental too all. In your time every human on earth was condemned to an eternal hell by at least one of these religions or splintered factions therein. This sort of thinking has also been removed. I believe that Matt already went into this with you folks. Religion is still here. Religious excesses have been removed. Now, remember—we still are unaware of what lies beyond that mysterious veil of that *Second Level.*"

The crew members remained focused on every word uttered by Colonel Caldwell, who continued saying:

"This is where the true deity may reveal itself. So all of us that believe in a particular God, may very well be proven psychic or correct at this time. Although, the odds of this being the case are very much against any one individual. Our great deity may prove to be a composite of many or all the gods of the great and near great religions. The deity may be totally alien to everything we've been taught, but—we here, in this time of human development, are convinced that such a presence does exist. There is no way that we mere mortals are the *ultimate* level of intellectual development. Even the most gifted among us cannot qualify as the final arbiter. God is there and will eventually be revealed to us all."

"Boy! That's a lot to swallow—all at once!" Rob Carmody studied the eyes of his instructor, searching for the truth.

"I understand your reaction Sergeant Carmody. We certainly don't expect you to reprogram your religious beliefs right now. Certainly not while sitting here. All that I want you and your friends here to do, is consider what I've said and discuss it among yourselves. Later, in future discussions with some of us 'Moderns' you'll probably come around, or at least modify your thinking when it comes to some of the excesses preached in your present religion."

Rob Carmody was non-committal in thought and expression concerning this. He had been indoctrinated in Catholic religious belief since early childhood. Yet, he did feel that there was a good deal of logic in the colonel's presentation.

"Now—in the area of Military Customs and Traditions, let me attempt to bring you all up to speed on where we now stand. As, I'm sure, all of you have noticed, we are no longer known as The United States Air Force. Same organization, different name. We aren't even know as the Aerospace Force. The word *force* has been removed from the title and the old designation *service* has been returned. Prior to World War Two, back in Billy Mitchell's time, we were the Air Service. Now we are the Aerospace Service."

"What was the motivation for the change, James?"

"Sure—let me explain Tom, and the rest of you. The word 'force' with all its power and threat connotations, is no longer needed. When the Air Force and the other military organizations were the only viable threat for retaliation against an enemy attack, the word force was proper. Today, such a word would give off a negative and completely incorrect connotation. We now are a 'service' for mankind in the areas of scientific exploration and space travel. No longer do our air crews head out on missions of destruction, and for this we thank the changes that I and your other instructors have referred to.

"This is not to denigrate in the least those brave air crews of the past that repeatedly risked their lives to protect this country and its allies. One can hardly imagine the courage that was displayed when these crew members again and again crawled into their aircraft to head out into enemy territory on reconnaissance and bombing missions. We also, should never forget Winston Churchill's *few.* They were those very brave young men who took their tiny fighter aircraft up to stop the Luftwaffe in the 'Battle of Britain' back in Nineteen Forty. However, the word force is no longer appropriate, whether it is the United States Air Force or Great Britain's Royal Air Force."

At this moment, a long silent Mathias Driscoll chimed in:

"Maybe even more enduring than the Rodney King quote that I alluded to earlier, was the Winston Churchill quote concerning that historic moment. If I remember my World War Two history lessons correctly, it went something like this: '*Never before in the field of human conflict was so much owed by so many, to so few.*'"

Matt then went on to say:

"It may have seemed like juvenile foolhardiness at first when those teenaged airmen climbed into their Spitfires and Hurricanes, but as their missions mounted up, it was simply raw courage. Many of these young men never celebrated their twenty-first birthdays."

"Thank you Captain for that rather eloquent touch of history," continued Colonel Caldwell.

"I fully concur… Now let me return to the subject of Customs and Traditions. You all are still under the legal boundaries and protections of 'The Uniform Code of Military Justice.' I'm certain that there have been numerous changes and interpretations of this code over the centuries, however, the basic framework remains. Many of these boundaries and protections are also found in the legal applications of civil law as well."

"Big Brother again Colonel?"

Janet had her hand up when she fired out her favorite reaction to the tighter controls she noticed in the civilian life of the "moderns."

"That's right Major—and remember, we all welcome said brother. This is not the infamous 'Big Brother' described by George Orwell in his novel *Nineteen Eighty-Four,* but is a much more benevolent brother carefully maintained by numerous controls. Of course I'm referring to the United Nations in Bern, Switzerland. One might consider that organizations' Secretary General as the ultimate 'Big Brother,' yet he an his subordinates are subject to immediate individual recall if it is determined by a majority of the public, through referendum, that any of them are guilty of overstepping their authority."

Lieutenant Colonel James Caldwell then proceeded to show the short holographic presentation on military-protocol, discipline and standards of behavior. There wasn't anything too shocking in this presentation, much of the etiquette was familiar to all. Items of *dress* and *appearance* were stressed, which fit with what the crew members had noticed about their military hosts. To a person their uniforms were neat and clean, as was their physical grooming. "Sharp" was the military term one used in referring to this sort of appearance. The military personnel of the Fourth Millennium were definitely *sharp.*

# CHAPTER ELEVEN

On Wednesday, April 22nd the crew had their next important briefing. It was only three days before setting off on their vacations. The title of this briefing was: "Political Indoctrination." Another neatly printed sign located on the door of their briefing room, announced this to all.

It was early on an overcast morning when the five astronauts entered the familiar briefing room. The ever-present marine-layer of thick fog covered the entire base and part of the nearby city, as it did on most mornings this time of year. They were greeted by Matt Driscoll and an attractive young woman in civilian clothes. Sergeant Carmody found it difficult to tell her age, a problem that he and the others found increasingly disconcerting in their dealings with other "Moderns."

Gina Krieger motioned for everyone to sit down after her introduction by Captain Driscoll. She had been introduced as the Senior United States Senator for California. Gina looked intently at her captive audience and began the lecture which was concerned with what had transpired politically during the past millennium, and what was going on now. Naturally, she could only cover the high points of this epic period. She was motivated to inform her little audience of the political situation before they left on *leave* Saturday morning. She rightfully concluded that they should be better equipped for the changes they were about to experience, so she made an effort to explain some of these difference in the brief time allotted.

Gina, like Matt Driscoll, was a history major in college. She informed her audience of this and mentioned that she had graduated from the University of Colorado at Boulder with a Masters Degree in

Public Administration as well as her BA in History. She received this final degree in 2992. This gave an indication of her age, which had appeared to the crew to be about forty, and now computed out to be a surprisingly youthful sixty. Her audience was very impressed that a United States Senator was called in to give the briefing. They were beginning to realize how important their arrival from the distant past was to the people of the Thirty-First Century.

"Let's keep this discussion informal, however, if you have a question I would appreciate it if you would please raise your hand."

Brice raised his hand immediately.

"Come on Colonel—I haven't even started. Alright, go ahead with your question."

"How do we rate the Senior Senator for this briefing? It seems to me that it's a little odd to have someone as exalted as you to brief our little crew."

"Exalted... There's your first mistake Colonel. Naturally things have changed significantly since you left. The days of members of congress being looked upon as exalted or any other similar adjective, are long gone. We now truly are the servants of the people and we take that phrase seriously. Now that we have already entered this part of my political presentation, let me continue on this subject."

Senator Gina Krieger now had the full attention and interest of her "Time-travelers."

"Congress in your time had become so corrupted by special-interest lobbyists that the peoples work was not being accomplished. This, along with party loyalties overriding the good of the nation, had dangerously lowered the publics view of both houses of Congress. It seemed to most citizens that only 'Con-Men' or *women* ran successfully for these offices. This proved to be true in some cases, however, there were more than a few truly noble politicians whose reputations were tarnished by the behavior of the many."

With this statement, Senator Krieger noted affirmative nods from her audience.

"Finally, laws were passed dealing with lobbyist and political party abuses. These became punishable crimes and the punishments were severe. The new laws were challenged, of course, yet it was quite an accomplishment that they were ever passed by the very institutions that they were meant to control. The word was out to beware of charismatic politicians. The voters finally became fed-up with the graft and came out to vote. Voter apathy had been one of the root causes of these problems. It was Twenty Thirty-Six when the makeup of congress changed enough to get these laws of reformation passed. I won't bore you with the details, suffice it to say that these were positive changes, and they still remained within the scope and intent of the Constitution. We now have a government far more reflective of what our founders had in mind."

The crew looked upon this last statement with some skepticism seeing that the presenter was herself a rather charismatic politician. The senator noted this subtle group reaction and continued:

"The pay schedules for congress-people were changed downward in relation to the buying power of the times. This was to further reflect the original plans of the 'Founders.' Congressional staffs have been dramatically reduced and the cost of doing the peoples business has dropped precipitously."

Lilly French's hand shot up on hearing this.

"Yes Sergeant French ?"

"With smaller congressional staffs, how are you able to take proper care of your constituents?"

"The staffs were badly bloated in the early Twenty-First Century. We now have so much automated equipment with immediate world-wide contact, that it is no longer necessary to have large staffs. Automation has replaced 'Empire building.' We still maintain staffs, however. I maintain an office here in the state capitol as well as in the national capitol in Denver. Our work load isn't as demanding as it was in your time. The citizenry is far more compliant now than it was then."

"Compliant… It sounds like 'Big Brother' again. It sounds like state control to me."

Janet Hulse's remarks were more like an outburst, and she had failed to raise her hand.

"Please Major, didn't I request that you raise your hand and be recognized before speaking."

There was a faint edge of threat in the Senator's remark. The others noted this as well as Janet, and at this moment Gina Krieger's warm presentation developed the chill of military authority. The senator slowly continued:

"I've read George Orwell's novel, therefore, I must state that we are a long way from an 'Orwellian Society.' Citizens world wide are well satisfied with the present political arrangements. Due to their sound Elementary and High School educations, they all have been made aware of the enormous difficulties faced by their ancestors.

"If I may use your first names for a moment… Tom—Janet—Rob—Norm—Lilly—forgive my admonishment of you Janet. Actually, I was making an example, there is a rather steely edge to our laws and practices. For the good of the *many*, of course."

Senator Krieger looked each crew member in the eye as she referred to them by their first names.

"Things are much different here than you folks are used to. Yes, the people *are* more compliant and submissive. However, there is good reason for this. As you have been told, we don't have much crime. We don't have any poverty or war. There is no great desire to gain more money because it won't buy people much more than they already have available. Unnatural greed has all but been eliminated from society and part of this is due to the altering of the 'Human Genome' in the area of compulsive behavior. As you have already learned, ostentation of any kind is abhorrent. For individuals or families to *show-off* their wealth is considered disgraceful behavior. Such lack of manners engenders great disrespect, which is just the opposite reaction intended. However, the lack of monetary incentives has posed a problem through the years, yet we have found the use of non-monetary awards and special recognition helped curb human greed. There still are varying standards of living, but they all are quite acceptable. One might say that we all have been *brain washed,* and we love it."

The five crew members thought about this, looked at one another, then shook their heads affirmatively. It did seem to make sense. You loose something to gain something else. In this case, the great human population of the suns third planet, gave up some of their cherished, often misused, freedoms to gain a better standard of living for all. Senator Gina Krieger's image now seemed to soften somewhat in the eyes of the travelers. There remained some nagging thoughts about possible misuse of power by the leaders. They all were aware of Plato's admonishment that absolute power corrupts—absolutely. As if she read their minds, the senator continued:

"Our leadership is well controlled with term-limits and a powerful recall plan that has become accepted, even institutionalized."

Norm Johnson's hand shot up at this and when recognized he asked:

"What are those 'Term-Limits,' Senator?"

"Twelve years, Sergeant Johnson, is as long as any elected member of Congress can serve. The Presidency is still two terms or eight years. That's two terms for a senator and six terms for a member of the House. That's total years, not just consecutive. Following this, the individual is retired at half pay, not full pay, as was the case in your time.

"Our politicians also have to pass stiff psychological testing before they can even run for office. You might find it amusing that they even have to make public their personal intelligence test results. This requirement was hit and miss for awhile, that is until the electorate became sophisticated enough to realize that the highest 'I. Q.' was not a very good indicator of leadership ability. Can you imagine Albert Einstein as the President…? However it is a good indicator for weeding out those that, quite frankly, were, or are, mentally or psychologically challenged. This is the accepted way to describe those who were dumb as hell or simply *nuts."*

This remark gained a collective laugh from the group, and they now were even more convinced that this brave new world might be on the proper track.

"The paranoid psychos are gone," continued Gina:

"I do, however, feel that we have paid a price for this compliance. Creativity may suffer, but let me remind you all of the problems with demanding unlimited individual freedom. Individual freedoms were not unlimited, yet many from your era considered that to be the case. When one's freedom of action impinges on another's freedom of action, the dilemma develops. This finally gave way to stricter rules of behavior and *compliance.*"

The crew now sat quietly in full compliance with the protocol of the briefing.

"We still have the United Nations," continued Gina Krieger.

"The decades of that institution's corruption and ineffectiveness are gone. The original idea of forming such a world organization, was correct. However, it took the disasters of the late Twenty-First and early Twenty-Second Centuries to truly straighten out that organization.

The United Nations ran the colossal relief efforts world wide. And, even though it took decades, the results were highly successful. Part of their success is why the entire planet now uses Megas as the symbol of monetary exchange. The United Nations is our treasury."

Rob suddenly raised his hand.

"Yes Sergeant Carmody, what do you have for us?"

"What about Language Senator? It seems to me that nothing could be more unifying than a universal language."

"We're working successfully on that one Sergeant. It had been tried before, back in the Nineteenth Century. I believe the proponents called it 'Esperanto.' It didn't take, however, the new approach has had much more success. For centuries English has been the prime language of business and wealth in the Western World. Prior to this, the controlling languages in the West were Greek, then came Latin, Spanish, French, Dutch, etcetera... The same sort of changes developed among the Eastern languages of Asia.

"The new approach calls for every child in their school systems world-wide to learn their own language and English simultaneously. We have been aware for some time that young children, in their first four years of school, are capable of learning two languages at the same time with remarkable fluency. You'll receive a complete briefing on our education system, which is now a world-wide system. I believe Michiko Trent will bring you all up to speed on this subject tomorrow."

The senator stopped for a moment and studied her audience, and she seemed to have read their collective minds when she continued:

"I know that you were aware of this ability of the young, back in your time. There is a difference now. We now have a higher level of education throughout the planet, thanks to some very sophisticated training devices, and a different attitude about school curriculum. Those children raised in an English speaking nation are *required* to become fluent in at least one other language of their choice. They all do, without exception, thanks to the training aides I just referred to. Most students add one or more new languages later on in high school and college. You'll find that you can now travel the world without the language barriers of the past. It is my feeling that all of you will probably be traveling throughout our little planet, as well as across our interesting solar system, in the very near future."

Tom Brice raised his hand. "Yes Colonel Brice."

"I understand why we annexed Mexico. I can see where it would help both nations and I could see it coming before we left. I wonder Senator—have there been any other similar annexations?"

"That's my next subject Colonel. Due to the size and destructive nature of the disasters, annexation became a viable, and in some cases, the only practical solution. Many small sea- side nations were almost totally wiped-out through inundation. Since the cooling period, that climaxed in the late Twenty-Second and early Twenty-Third Centuries, some of these lands have been reclaimed. However, the great national combines created through the survival efforts of the United Nations have remained. Even the United Nations had to seek a new home and is presently located in Bern, Switzerland. I say presently, yet it's been at this *new* home for over seven hundred years. Most of the one hundred and ninety-seven recognized independent nations of the Twenty-First Century remain as semi-autonomous states. Some have disappeared, but most remain much as our seventy-one states."

Sergeant Johnson raised his hand.

"Yes Sergeant."

"What about Canada Senator? If this is true why isn't Canada a part of the United States of America? Why isn't Canada a part of the United States of *North* America?"

"We're also still working on that one Sergeant. There are some nations that didn't want to join up in these powerful groupings and Canada and Russia are two of them. We feel that those independent countries, being physically the two largest independent countries on earth at that time, had something to do with it. Furthermore, Russia didn't want to return to its negative memories of the old Soviet Union, nor, more importantly, neither did its neighbors care to go back to those unpleasant days."

Sergeant Johnson rolled his eyes, then remarked:

"We'll, I can understand not wanting to become part of a large conglomerate."

The senator smiled and continued:

"There are 'The Free States of Central America,' 'The Unified States of South America,' and 'The European Union.' I believe that The European Union was well along by the time you departed. Most of the rest of the world is divided up in a similar fashion and at the end of this briefing I'll provide handouts explaining this in detail. None of the individual states are required to maintain armed forces which provides a considerable savings for their people. All of the united groupings are democracies and all provide properly for their citizenry. Each united grouping also provides, through the U.N., some special trade or resource, that is indigenous to their area, into the world-wide trade. This trade is regulated by the U.N. and credits developed are properly weighted and distributed. This provides a higher standard of living for all, and if it seems too good to be true—it isn't. I'm happy to tell you that it finally works."

Lilly French now raised her hand and was recognized by the senator.

"What about political parties Senator? Do we still have Republicans and Democrats?"

"Yes we do Sergeant. We also have a powerful third party, the 'Liberty Party.' I believe that this was known as the Libertarian Party in your time. Since then it has developed into a viable and highly competitive third party, and all political discourse started to be aimed at what was good for the nation. The party leaderships found it difficult to aim negative advertising at two powerful targets. They started pushing their advertising resources at what was best for the Nation. They found that the public didn't accept having both 'out-of-power' parties aiming their defamations at those 'in-power.' Somehow this was not considered the 'American Way.' When those who weren't 'in-office' aimed their criticism at actual problems and articulated possible solutions, they found success. Presently the Liberty Party controls both houses of congress and the Presidency. Also, political advertising is tightly controlled with equal television time to the leading candidates, and this TV time is limited."

"What party are you Senator?"

Tom asked this question without going through the formality of raising his hand.

Senator Krieger now paid no attention to this slight breach of etiquette, and replied:

"I'm a member of the Liberty Party Colonel… Thanks for asking."

Rob Carmody now raised his hand and when recognized asked:

"What finally works Senator? A moment ago you said that the system finally works. I think I understand the three party system, yet I'm not sure that I follow that whole system. It sure sounds like Socialism to me, and how do you decide an election when there isn't a clear majority? Do you have to go through the expense of a 'run-off?' How do you divided up the electoral votes in a national election?"

"Whoa! One at a time please, Sergeant Carmody. First, you mentioned electoral votes referring to the Electoral College. The Electoral College was archaic in your time, following the arrival of mass electronic communications. It was out of touch with reality and if it still existed, it would be criminal. I realize that in the Eighteenth and Nineteenth Centuries such a system was necessary due to the horse and buggy lifestyle, but not now. It should have gone out with hoop skirts."

"Hoop skirts are out?" responded Carmody.

"Very funny Sergeant. The Electoral College was finally scrapped near the middle of your Twenty-First Century. Elections, both national and local, are simply decided on the numbers. The leading vote getter wins—no overall majority is required."

"Excuse me Senator, what about fraud?"

This was Rob's immediate response as Senator Krieger finished her explanation on the demise of the old electoral system.

"Fraud is rather difficult today, think about it. How can there be fraud when they no longer allow absentee balloting and everyone is identity scanned at the polls. That means that their identity implants are scanned and checked against their personal identification cards. By the way, this process takes about one second. The same process is used when boarding aircraft or any other time when such security is required.

"Now, to answer you initial question. What finally works Sergeant isn't classical Socialism. What finally works is that we have reached a system of *nearly* equal distribution of goods and services for all, while maintaining incentives for innovation and accomplishment. There are varied standards of living. The variations just aren't as wide as they were in your time. The distance between the wealthy and the rest has been narrowed considerably, yet not enough to destroy innovation. Just because our citizens of today don't have obsessive monetary goals for their accomplishments, doesn't mean they don't strive just as hard for perfection.

"Now, my brave travelers, isn't anybody going to ask about taxation? I thought that this would have been one of your initial questions. I realize from my studies of American History that back in your time you had to put up with rather regressive income taxes. I believe that you also had sales taxes and a host of hidden taxes. Seeing that our present government payrolls are much smaller than they were in your time and seeing that we have little crime, less demand on a military, and greatly reduced medical costs—a small sales tax of five percent on all goods and services, is sufficient to run all levels of government. Individuals still pay into a Social Security Fund, but even that bite is far less than in your time. Are there any questions about taxes?"

Tom Brice raised his hand then offered:

"Madam Senator—this five percent sales tax thing still seems regressive by putting an unfair burden on those less able to pay for these 'goods and services' than on the wealthy. Shouldn't the wealthy have to pay a greater share?'

"Come on Colonel, remember that we have closed the huge disparity chasm. It is now merely a tiny, easily forded stream. Those individuals with larger incomes normally buy a few more goods and services and, therefore, they do pay more taxes."

"What about 'Death Taxes Senator?'" asked Janet.

"We've had some problems with this in our family concerning some of my grandparents property, when they died."

"That's the big one Major. That's the big change, and you probably won't welcome the answer. Anyway, here it is:

"When an individual dies, a property settlement is established by the State Board, using very specific guidelines that come from Bern. These guidelines are rather complex, however I have a handout for you all concerning this. I feel that it will be many years before such an event would involve you healthy looking specimens. Anyway—the Board will determine what passes to the surviving spouse and then to the surviving children. Even if the surviving spouse is near the top of the 'Wealth Scale' in their own right, only certain heirlooms pass along with their Life-Lease. Another change is that there is no individual ownership of 'real-property.' The public at large owns all the land and the improvements thereon. Now, if the surviving child or children involved require some financial assistance, it is provided. If it involves the death of the last spouse, their Life-Lease may pass to the children, depending on age. I believe that this is similar to some of the laws from some of the states back in you time. Now—it's universal."

"No private ownership of real property Senator? You're telling us that that's not Communism? That's the very definition of Communism. We all are educated people and we knew that this present system was Socialism… but now it seems to be Communistic."

As soon as Janet made this remark the others agreed with "right-on," or just a nodding of agreement. She and the others were again surprised at their rather tepid reaction to the fact that they now figured their beloved country had slid into that despised form of government.

"I figured that this would become a sore point for all of you when we approached the subject of ownership of real property, continued the senator. Back in your time, the highest percentage of private wealth was in real estate. This naturally involved huge holdings of the very wealthy. It seems that in the Twenty-First Century eighty-six percent of the worlds wealth was controlled by five percent of the population. Not only was this unfair and unnatural, it bordered on criminal. Since the disasters of the Twenty-Second Century, that situation has changed and now all of the real property of this planet is owned by all of the people—*equally.*"

"I guess we'll have to get used to that one, now, how about young children Senator…? What about surviving young children?"

"Even less likely Major Hulse, however, the state would make arrangements for their care, probably through other family members and the Life-Leases on real-property that then would revert, or escheat, to the State."

"Why less likely Senator?"

"Accidental or premature medical deaths are extremely rare in today's society. Remember—no wars, safety controlled transportation, no diseases, improved medical technology…"

"Senator—who gets the money that's left over when a quote 'fairly wealthy' individual dies. You just said that the different levels of government perform well on the five percent sales tax. Who gets these '*Death-Taxes?*'"

"Good one Rob. That money goes into the National Education Fund and is used to cover the expenses of building or refurbishing our school system. The financial records of this organization are quite transparent so, once again, no fraud."

"Alright Senator, that seems to answer some of our questions concerning Real-Property. What about bank accounts and stocks and bonds? What about financial wealth?"

"This is the crux of this discussion Colonel. We are a society that has come to the understanding that great personal wealth is a detriment to an orderly society. In the Nineteenth and Twentieth Centuries, people looked upon the wealthy as special, and displays of wealth were often viewed as a positive thing. This was even true among the common people. They made heroes out of the wealthy no matter how illogical that was. To make heroes out of the accomplished is one thing, and this still remains. Making heroes of those who are merely wealthy has disappeared. The State Board determines exactly how much of the deceased's wealth will pass, and that is it. The rest goes to the National Education Fund. By the way Colonel, there no longer are such things as *stocks and bonds.*"

"Then Senator, this really is a Communist society, isn't that so?"

"We are still a Democracy Colonel. We hope we have finally avoided the disparities and excesses of the past. As I have explained, we have tight controls on our elected officials which has *eliminated* graft and fraud. There's no great incentive for these vices any longer. Everyone's standard of living is quite high. The original promise of Socialism was spelled out as a sort of *Nirvana* by Marx and Engles, but as we now are well aware, this became impossible to achieve. Greed rose an ugly specter in every social experiment. Russia tried Communism which gave ownership of everything to the state. This totally destroyed incentive, yet provided wealth for a controlling greedy few. Then, capitalism, brought in entrepreneurial genius and with it huge technological, industrial, and economic advances. However, a very large portion of the world's population was left out of the increased wealth. This is where the term, 'The Third World,' originated.

"We now believe that with our controls, our distribution system, and our human engineering, we are making it work. We don't call it Communism or Socialism any longer. The entire population of this planet enjoys what we now refer to as a *Social Democracy...*"

"No stocks and bonds, no stock market—who owns all the business's? Not the United Nations again."

"We all do Janet, and yes this is controlled by the 'Business Management Division' of the United Nations at Bern."

"What about the lazy, Senator? What about those people who refuse to pull their weight? What about people who refuse to work?"

"Very rare, Colonel Brice. Psychologically we have been raised to 'pull our weight,' as you put it. Not to do this would engender great disrespect, even enmity from the rest of society. If such behavior could not be corrected with the proper admonitions, it would lead to a brain scan of the individual involved. Following this would be recommendations by a certified medical board on what implants would be required to reach compliance. All our citizens are well aware of this. These situations, however, are extremely rare."

"Yes… I can imagine that they are," responded Colonel Tom Brice.

"Just one more question Senator."

"Go ahead Colonel."

"If the United Nations in Bern, Switzerland has so much power and control -- what then do our elected officials do?"

Senator Krieger looked as if she expected this question and carefully stated:

"We establish local policy and provide local assistance. Different parts of the globe have different problems and demands due to the great variations in physical and climatic situations. This requires more flexibility than one might think."

"You say 'local policy' and 'local assistance,' meaning, I presume, local -- state -- and federal? What about our National Constitution, Senator? Have we turned our national independence over to an outside entity -- The United Nations?"

"To answer your question rather succinctly -- Yes. We all have Colonel."

Senior Senator Gina Krieger once again eyed each of her attentive charges individually, then slowly and distinctly said:

"May I be so bold as to now announce that despite this little shocker, things are really great here in this Fourth Millennium!"

# CHAPTER TWELVE

At dinner that evening the "Five" were joined once more by Matt Driscoll who naturally sat next to Lilly "Red" French. He had become fascinated by her pale white skin and beautiful dark red hair. Matt had experienced plenty of success with attractive women, yet he had never developed the same feelings that he now had for this bright and pleasant young lady. He was also aware that she was a Master Sergeant which might cause some protocol problem in the future. They were both about the same age and the commissioned officer versus non-commissioned officer problem seemed minor. In fact it had little or no bearing on his developing ardor.

He wasn't sure how Lilly felt about him and it seemed to him that she maneuvered away from conversations that might lead to discussions about the two of them. It was here, in the Vandenberg Officers Club, that he became aware that he was very much in love with Lilly, and he felt that he would eventually possess her. He further imagined that such an arrangement would soon become permanent.

Lilly looked into the strong handsome face of her benefactor, staring unflinchingly into his bright blue eyes. She continued to stare unabashedly at him and soon they both broke out laughing. At that moment she knew how he felt. Not a word was said, but the sparring was over and they both knew it. She reached for and caught his left hand under the table without the rest of the crew being aware. She squeezed and he squeezed back, which, for the two of them, was tantamount to a formal pledge of unity.

The discussion about the weeks briefings as well as their trip to Santa Maria continued among the crew as they faced each other across the large oval table. Lilly joined in, as if nothing had happened between her and Matt. The others had seen the look and the laugh, so their secret was about as well concealed as Tom and Janet's before their little announcement had been made during the bus ride to Santa Maria.

"It still seems like old fashioned Socialism," Lilly chimed in as the discussion moved to their most recent briefing. She made this remark as if nothing at all had transpired between herself and Matt.

"I don't know what to tell you Sergeant," responded Matt in a rather formal tone, which did little to hide what had just happened between he and Lilly. They both seemed a little flustered as they vainly attempted to shield their emotions from their companions.

"I've lived under this system all my life so I guess I'll have to stay out of this conversation."

"Come on Matt—cut the crap. Why are you calling Lilly, Sergeant. We know you're nuts about her, plus were all sitting here in civilian clothes. No military ranks—understood?"

"Yes Sir Colonel, oops—, I mean Tom."

With this, everyone at the table laughed and the rest of the dinner turned into a very pleasant affair. Following the fine meal and after a few glasses of the local wine, Rob and Norm decided to move over to the bar. The not so subtle behavior of the two couples was beginning to wear on the *single* sergeants. They were both happy for the lovers, but they knew they wouldn't be missed as they excused themselves and left the table. They weren't.

Both Rob and Norm were becoming aware that their unusual appearance was not going to be much of a hindrance when it came to being accepted by members of the opposite sex among the moderns. They realized that much of this acceptance was based on curiosity, but that certainly didn't cause either of them any regrets in their dealings with the beautiful young female officers of the fourth millennium.

* * *

The next morning the sign on the door announced: EDUCATION SYSTEM.

Matt Driscoll, as usual, introduced the morning's briefer as Michiko Trent. The crew recognized the Japanese first name but could not identify any Asiatic features in the pretty young woman. After further study they realized that the features were there. They were quite subtle, and as they now understood, were incorporated into the appearance of every "Modern." The crew members had also become aware that many of the old names had persisted through the centuries, and Michiko, a very popular name in Japan during their time, was one such name. Michiko was a school board executive and a teacher in the Vandenberg school system.

"Good morning my traveler friends—welcome. Now, let me try to bring you all up to speed concerning the present state of our education system."

"Do you mean here at Vandenberg, or worldwide, Madam?"

Michiko Trent smiled at Tom Brice's question and replied, "There both the same thing Colonel. Now, if you please, I'll begin.

"First I'll discuss with you the present days school curriculum and also some of the teaching aides that I believe have been referenced in your previous briefings. We still have Pre-School for children ranging from four years old up to seven."

This statement brought an immediate response:

"I thought your system was more advanced. Seven seems a little regressive for Pre-School."

Michiko smiled at Janet's response and continued:

"The reason Pre-School lasts three years and includes some seven year olds, is that our upper levels are quite a lot more accelerated than in your time. We don't want children too young and immature to be exposed to the higher levels that they will receive by the time the reach High School. Children are not allowed to enter Elementary School until they have passed their seventh birthday. Questions…?"

"We've been told that by seven these children have mastered an additional language. How is this possible when we know that students of this age are barely able to read and write in their native language. Please explain how these modern students are able to read and write a foreign language by their seventh birthdays?"

The other crew members stared at Michiko, waiting for an answer to Norm Johnson's provocative question.

"When you were told that these young children had become fluent in another language, this meant conversationally fluent. This is accomplished through sound recordings and holographic presentations. These presentations are universal for each language that has been retained, therefore, pronunciation and usage are universal."

"Question Miss Trent." Lilly leaned forward and asked: "Each Language *retained*…? Please explain."

"Certainly! Of the approximately twenty-eight hundred languages that existed on the planet in your time, only fifteen have been retained as principle languages. That's *fifteen* total—not fifteen hundred. Many of these languages are language groupings such as German, which includes Dutch, Austrian and Danish, while Japanese includes Korean. Nordic is a composite language which includes Norwegian, Swedish and Finish. Russian is spoken in the old Baltic states, and so on. Having fifteen international languages is certainly easier for travel and trade. English is prime!"

Michiko studied the calm expressions of the astronauts upon receiving this information, and rightfully surmised that they were naturally content with this arraignment, seeing that English was their principle language. She then continued:

"Valid arguments have been made over the years that Italian, Spanish and French were, or indeed are, the most expressive and lyrical languages, and that German and Japanese are the most analytical and precise. However, business and trade seems to trump all these other reasons, so English it is. There is also the compelling argument that English is the most dynamic, and has by far the largest vocabulary. I believe that you have been filled in on the fact that English has become the true International Language, while the other fourteen are retained in their varied parts of the globe. Most children have mastered three languages by the time they graduate from High School."

"Why retain the others if English is the true international language?" Lilly's question was seconded by the others.

"Because, Sergeant *French*, there is a long history of great literature in these other languages. That seems like a rather surprising question coming from someone with your last name. Furthermore, we certainly cannot overlook the magnificent songs and operatic arias that exist in many languages. We feel, and have noticed, that there often is a loss of meaning or poetic flair when great works are translated into English.

And with the music, just imagine those Italian Operas being sung in English. Boy—that thought brings on a chill of discomfort.

"The rest of it has to do with customs and traditions in the host countries. Some of those original twenty-eight hundred languages are still passed on to new generations through their individual cultures. These languages certainly are not outlawed, however they are no longer recognized in international dealings. Of course, most of these lesser known languages were never used internationally.

"Anyway, children are retained in Pre-School until they've reached the age of seven. Because of the curriculum there, they are educated well beyond the original 'baby sitting' concept of *Kindergarten*. Pre-School is not just learning a second language. We also provide instruction in basic math, and just as important, we teach the children how to interact with one another. Naturally, they have plenty of games and team sports to occupy their great supply of energy. Don't we all wish we could bottle that childhood attribute up and use it throughout our lives. Pre-School is a 'good-time' as I'm sure it was in your past."

"This language thing sounds like a better arrangement for worldwide communications," offered Tom Brice.

"However, I bet it really pissed-off some other countries—especially the French and Spanish, and of course, Chinese."

"Not really Colonel, this transition didn't happen all at once, or by a United Nations edict. It happened gradually over many centuries and when the U. N. decided on English as the international business language, it had already been this for many years. Actually, there may be more people fluent in French, Spanish, and Chinese today than ever before. This despite the dramatic drop in the world's population due to the disasters that I believe you've been briefed about. This, naturally, is due to expanded formal multi-language training.

"Now let's move on, and into the Elementary School ages and that curriculum. In the area of language—this is where the students perfect their grammar and writing abilities. This is true for both English and their second language, which out here in California is normally Spanish. These skills are more fully developed in First through Third Grade, or ages seven through nine. By completion of Third Grade, the modern student has become competent and even creative in both languages. During these same three grades the students Math skills are developed in the area of basic Arithmetic. History is also explored in these three years. American History is the principle area of study here, but this requires some basic courses in Ancient History to give the student grounding concerning human development.

"Ancient, European, and Asian History will be explored in greater detail as the students move forward into the second half of Elementary School. Now that they have reached a level of competency in basic math, they are introduced to science courses during this same period. This, of course, includes Fourth through Sixth Grade and students aged ten through twelve."

"Is that the extent of Elementary School? Is it the same as we had with Middle School being next?"

Rob studied Michiko when he continued:

"There doesn't seem anything too unusual in this—so far."

"It's the *so far* Sergeant Carmody, that might indicate some difference. As I mentioned, when our students enter the Fourth Grade, they are well rounded in basic Math. In Fourth Grade they take on Pre-Algebra, then Algebra and Geometry in the Fifth and Sixth, leaving them open to Calculus in their Middle-School Seventh Grade and Differential Calculus in their Eighth Grade."

"Wow! I see what you mean," responded Rob.

"Differential Calculus at thirteen and fourteen years old. That's quite a leap."

"Not really Sergeant, we have found that thirteen and fourteen year old students, with their uncluttered minds can grasp and fully understand some of the most obscure and convoluted concepts when it comes to Math and Science."

With this last remark, Michiko ushered in four Middle-School students who had been waiting out in the hall. She then introduced the two girls and two boys to the crew members. They represented both of the grades at their school. Following the introduction, the crew members were told that they could ask the young people about their school and their education in general. All the crew members joined in, as did all the students. The adults were surprised, even startled by the quick articulate and knowledgeable responses of the students. They were also impressed with the students comfortable demeanor in discussing these things with five strange visitors from the past. These interviews continued for some time, until finally Michiko held up her hand and said:

"That's enough—thanks kids, you did very well."

The five crew members stood up and applauded the attractive young people for their fine effort. After they left the room, Michiko turned back to her charges and said:

"Any questions?"

"What's left for High School? What the heck is left for College if they are already that far along when the finish Middle-School?"

"Good question Sergeant French, and that's what we'll discuss next—if you all will stay with me! Now, I think all would agree that it's time to take a break."

During the break period and while holding his hot cup of coffee, Norm Johnson leaned over the folding table, which was covered with trays of inviting delicacy's and said:

"I'm a little bit concerned with the way that this education thing is going. We all have fairly extensive education credentials from out time, yet these Middle-School students of today have already moved well beyond my level. Christ! I never had Differential Calculus."

"I wouldn't worry too much about that Norm," responded Tom Brice. "Differential Calculus is a course for Science and Engineering students. It's a specialized course and far from the requirements of most disciplines."

"That's what I thought Boss, but Michiko has implied that all 'modern' students complete this course by age fourteen. You saw it when we questioned these students. You asked them some questions about Calculus. What's most scary to me is that their answers seem to be correct. You had Calculus, were their answers correct?"

"Yes Norm—I'll have to admit that their answers were not only correct, but precise."

"That's my problem Boss. I'm a little worried that we all are going to be looked upon as those *dummies* from back in the Twenty-First Century!"

Following this thought provoking little gem, the five returned to their seats and Michiko Trent.

"Now let's see what goes on in the modern High School."

Michiko's opening remark drew a soft sigh of apprehension from some of the crew.

"First, when the children arrive at High School from Middle-School, they are considered to be well educated, as you have just witnessed, in the basics of two languages, plus Math, History and Science. They also have been well trained in much of the Arts and have already had extensive Physical Education training. Now, it is the job of the High Schools to proceed in greater depths in these disciplines while adding Government, Economics and Psychology."

"Psychology… Now, that really is a college course," remarked Janet Hulse.

"As a matter of fact, that's often Grad-school level."

"This is basic Psychology Major. These courses are a long way from the medical requirements that you may be referring too."

Michiko continued:

"In Government they learn about Local, State and National Governments, as well as the varied functions of the United Nations in Bern. They are informed about how these different organizations interact with each other in order to make our lives more pleasant and meaningful. During their three years in High School our children really grow. That is, they grow physically, mentally and emotionally.

"Yes Sergeant Carmody. Your question?"

"High School is now only three years. That seems to me to be a great deal of information to be passing on in just three years."

"Our students attend school eleven months a year, as opposed to nine months in your time. The Japanese and some of the Europeans used an eleven month school year back then, and their students were far better educated. Right now, all annual school holidays add up to no more than one month per year. Three times eleven means thirty three months of High School. Four times nine meant thirty-six months of High School in your era. If you then figure in attendance hours per day, we're then about equal. Then you have to add in the increased discipline in our classrooms, that gives a big edge to the present system. On top of that, you must then take into consideration our more advanced training tools such as some of the Holographic Presentations that you have recently seen, and other more advanced training aides that we posses—there's no longer any comparison."

"What are these training aides Miss Trent? We've heard you and others refer to them."

"Good question Sergeant French. Actually, it isn't really training aides plural, it's a system. Folks in your day were already experimenting with this concept. However, now the idea has been perfected. We have small recording discs about half the size of your old CD's. Each one of them can hold twenty gigabytes of information. These are what our children refer to as 'Dream Discs,' for they operate when they are asleep. They are normally set for one hour of operation, such as between three and four AM. The battery operated player is programmed to play just this long even though a single disc may hold an entire course of study."

"Hold on Miss Trent! Couldn't this cause some serious sleep deprivation in these young students? It seems to me that there could be some serious negative results from this."

"There were some problems in the early years of this teaching technique, Sergeant Carmody. These problems have been ironed out. This technique doesn't cause repetitious sound bytes as it did in the unit's infancy. It provides the sleeping student with full color images of the particular subject being taught. These are not harsh or disturbing images, instead rather pleasant and yet very informative presentations. The producers of these training aides have, with proper United Nations budgeting for these lessons, been able to make them very informative and quite entertaining. I'm sure that you all will be able to experience these little discs yourselves. This may help with any apprehensions that you may have about being educationally left behind. Many of these lessons are designed for adults as well as children."

Again an inaudible sigh of relief could be felt among the small crew.

"Please don't ask me how they get these beautiful mental pictures transferred into the brains of our sleeping children. I'm not a Neuro-Surgeon, however this does require an additional transplant just below the right ear."

"What? Another transplant. I fear that you all just may be turning into some sort of controlled androids!"

"Just take it easy Sergeant Johnson. Your probably right about one thing. If there was an overall evil intent by the authorities, this is probably how they would do it. It wouldn't avail any such group of controlling individuals to exist in our modern society seeing that everyone has pretty much what the desire when it comes to material goods. This coupled with the fact that there is no more insanity—at least clinical insanity. I should add that I don't think that there is…"

Michiko made eye contact with each of the crew members in turn following this last remark, then forced an evil grin as she crossed her eyes.

The crew members grasped the humor, yet there was a hint of fear in some of them. They were all very much aware that the implant that had sterilized them had also placed some furtive confines on their emotional responses to things that might have caused them greater aggravation in the past. They collectively felt that already their individual "free-thinking" had been somewhat compromised.

"By the time our students are seventeen," continued Michiko Trent, they are fully educated when it comes to general knowledge. From here they go on to University and from then on their education becomes more specialized. They have now entered the fields in which they've shown the greatest natural aptitude."

"What about children that just don't measure up scholastically? What happens to the students that are just naturally slow? What about these Miss Trent?"

"These are very rare cases today Sergeant French, but they do exist. We have a few 'Special Schools' throughout the country. Remember—there no longer are any physiologically retarded young people unless the have suffered after-birth brain injuries. These individuals are placed in a controlled environment, whether they are young or mature. The State takes care of all of the costs, which is not a very great burden seeing so few individuals are involved."

"Miss Trent—are these special individual aptitudes that you spoke of, revealed through testing?"

"Not really Colonel Brice, although that's one possible tool. That little implant just below the right ear, that I spoke of, can also be used to determine exactly what advanced training or specialized education the student is suited for. At seventeen years of age, we already know if a particular young person will be a Doctor, a Lawyer, or maybe an Indian Chief. There's not much call for the later in today's economy, but there are unlimited employment opportunities for our young people following their education. Most manual-labor jobs have disappeared, thanks to advances in robotics. This certainly applies to heavy, dangerous, boring, repetitious and otherwise demeaning types of labor.

"Now, if there are no more questions, that's all I have for you. I would like to thank you all for being a very attentive audience. Please, don't any of you worry about the possible inadequacies of your former educations. With what I've seen here today, and with your questions to me and especially with your questions to the children, I feel that you have nothing to worry about in you interactions with us 'Moderns.'"

Michiko Trent then turned the meeting back over to Matt Driscoll saying:

"I now leave this meeting in the very capable hands of Captain Driscoll."

* * *

Mathias Driscoll was born in Riverside, Connecticut, in 3001. This was a small village located within the township of Greenwich on the northern edge of Long Island Sound. During the disasters it had disappeared beneath fathoms of salt water as the Atlantic Ocean rolled across Long Island and into some of the low lying lands of New England. Following the "cooling period," many of the coastal towns and villages on this part of the continent were rebuilt and reoccupied.

Matt received his high school diploma from Saint Luke's School in nearby New Canaan. That school and town survived the floods being located on higher ground and further inland than Riverside. Following this, Matt was accepted at the venerable Air Service Academy which was still set dramatically against the eastern slope of the Rocky Mountains north of picturesque Colorado Springs. He eventually graduated near the top of his class in the year 3023. Beer drinking, party minded Matt, was fondly remembered by his class-mates as "Daring Driscoll" for his escapades as the rowdy tight-end of the national championship "Falcons" football team. Mathias Driscoll had always proven to be a very popular fellow as well with his young female counterparts at the Academy.

Captain Matt Driscoll had never let his previous relationships with young women become too serious. They were often romantic and sexually fulfilling interludes, yet he found that he was able to continuously shield himself from deeper and more profound liaisons. To his own wonderment and apprehension, this was no longer the case.

# CHAPTER THIRTEEN

THE FOLLOWING MORNING MATT escorted Lilly to the local art gallery in Santa Maria, at her request. Lilly, as a photographer and partially trained art student, wanted to see what sort of creativity remained in the artwork of the Moderns. As mentioned, Lilly French suffered from a fairly common form of color-blindness. It was the "red-green shift" variety which allowed her to view most of the color spectrum with the same accuracy as her fellow humans. When it came to *reds* she could see some shades and could even see well into the infra-red portion of the spectrum. It was the *greens* that she found to be the most problem. When she viewed painted greens, she viewed these as shades of gray. When it came to foliage, the greens recorded as browns on her sensitive retinas.

"Great for spotting camouflage," she would jokingly remark when asked about this handicap.

Actually, this visual "limitation" had become an aid in spotting an enemies camouflaged positions during the wars of the Twentieth Century. Lilly had been properly placed in the "war-time" Air Force as an aerial-rated still photographer.

Despite this minor limitation, Lilly enjoyed colorful artistic displays. She was able to perform her considerable talent in black and white charcoal sketching and still enjoyed viewing the colorful paintings of others.

Matt used a small Motor-Pool vehicle for this trip. There was room for four passengers, yet they were the only occupants. There was a steering wheel as well as an accelerator along with the necessary gauges, however, Lilly noticed that Matt still spoke to the vehicle and told it where to go. It responded smoothly after complying verbally to his request. Following his brief commands, the two passengers were able to sit back with their arms around each other.

"I knew it would be like this with you," said Lilly squeezing her lover's waist with ardor.

The real passion had been the previous night and early that morning. Their sexual enthusiasm was free and uninhibited while staying at Matt's little on-base apartment in the Single Officers Billet.

"I feel the same way Sweetheart. It's only you for me now, and from this moment on. I can't even imagine being with another woman. I guess you're stuck with me Lilly. I was in love with you before last night, so you didn't have to be such a great lover—but you are. God! I can't believe my luck."

When they arrived at the parking lot near the art gallery, Matt helped his Lilly from their little bus, then walked hand in hand with her to the entrance of the gallery. Lilly noticed the paintings in the large show window, and for an instant was returned to her century.

"These are copies of works from the Nineteenth and Twentieth Centuries, I recognize them. Degas, Picasso, Monet… there's Rembrandt and of course, Vincent Van Gough."

"That's right Sweetheart, the work of later artists is inside including some originals."

As the two proceeded through the large gallery, Lilly became less anxious concerning the possible stifling of the artistic output of this compliant society. Her fears continued to dissipate as she studied the bold and colorful paintings of the more recent artists. Much of the art work was dramatic and she voiced her approval. She compared some of the paintings to her favorite style which was the work of the "French Impressionists." She then realized that many of these artists must have been positively influenced by the old schools of the Nineteenth Century. There also were many new and delightful styles and she began to feel that life in this millennium might just be alright.

"What about music Matt? I prefer classical music. Have the *classics* persisted?"

"Yes—of course Sweetheart. My taste runs the same as yours in music, art and everything else for that matter!"

"You've figured all that out in just a week. Rather naïve of you big boy. I'm sure we'll disagree about many things. We're not clones either you know. I think you're just agreeing with me because you love me—right?"

"Of course! You obviously know more about these things than I do Lilly. Teach me pretty lady. Teach me more about art. Part of my college course of study included Art Appreciation, but listening to you, I fear that it wasn't very well presented. Maybe I'm a bit of a dunce when it comes to this subject, yet I do understand what your saying about these paintings and I always did like the work from your time as much as the work of our present artists. However, my taste in music really does run to the classical. Teach me more about art Darling, then my personal world with you beside me—really will be complete."

* * *

Friday afternoon, on the day prior to their departure for the nations capitol, the crew of "Aag-one" as it was now referred to, sat in the Vandenberg Operations Coffee Shop and discussed their upcoming "leave." They all realized that they hadn't been given much choice on where they would spend their thirty day vacation. Only Tom Brice's home town was spared from the disasters, yet some of the areas where they had been raised had been rebuilt following the Mini-Ice-Age of the late Twenty-Second and early Twenty-Third Centuries. As Major Hansen's disturbing holograph presentation had illustrated, their home towns, as well as most everyone's, had been abandoned to the seas. Some remained below newly formed lakes, while most were relocated to higher ground. They all had decided that to try to return to these areas would simply be exercises in futility. The old adage, "You cant go home," once again found its way into their conversation. The decision had been made collectively; they all would go to Denver.

"What are we going to do when we get there? Should we stay together? Boss,

It's your town. We'll let you show us around, how about that?"

"It's alright with me Rob, however, from what they have said, I doubt that I will know my way around. Blind leading the blind, and all that."

The ever present Matt Driscoll joined in:

"Come on folks, we're not just going to dump you all on the streets of Denver. Hell, I know my way around the capitol. I'll be there... Isn't that so Lilly?"

"Damned right!"

"Also, I can tell you now. We all have an important meeting to attend in Denver, tomorrow at noon. I can't tell you any more than that, but you all are expected."

"What sort of a meeting is this? What if some of us had picked different cities? What would you have said then Matt?"

Lilly French looked at the others as she questioned her man.

Matt smiled and responded to his lady while looking at each of his charges one at a time:

"I would have tried feebly to change your minds and persuade you all to go to Denver. Do you believe that I have such ability Lilly? You know—, the ability to be just a little persuasive."

"Alright Mathias... You've made your point."

* * *

It was Saturday morning the 25$^{th}$ of April when Matt Driscoll and the five travelers boarded their transport on the tarmac just west of Vandenberg Flight Operations. All of them were in a good mood as they set off on their 30 day vacation. Shortly afterward, their swept winged jet powered airplane whipped across the coastal ranges and the passengers were surprised to find out that even this small ten passenger local transport was fueled by anti-matter. There remained four empty seats as the six of them were the only passengers on this flight east. There was only a light buzzing from the two engines as they sped east towards Denver. Unlike the small busses that took them around the base and over the hills to Santa Maria, this aircraft had a pilot and even a co-pilot.

As their sleek little transport crossed Central California at sub-sonic speed, the space adventurers were able to notice some of the profound changes that had taken place since leaving their hidden base in Nevada one thousand years earlier. The most disturbing sight below them was Lake San Joaquin. The southern portion of this huge body of water was bordered by the Tehachapi Hills. Their flight plan for Denver took them directly over the place once occupied by the bustling city of Bakersfield. It was now a wide blue lake extending north to the very limits of their vision, even at their altitude of fifteen thousand feet.

"How far north does this extend?"

Tom "Boss" Brice asked the question that filled the thoughts of his other crew members.

Matt Driscoll turned towards his new found friends, hesitated for a brief instant, then responded:

"It extends north to San Francisco Bay. However, the hilly parts of San Francisco survived that early Twenty-Second Century disaster, along with the Oakland Hills. This great body of water is called a lake, but it actually is a vast bay or inland sea made up primarily of saltwater. Our geologists explained that this had been a sea millions of years earlier. This had been proven, even in your time, by the fossils found throughout the San Joaquin Valley floor. When the water receded during the cooling period, this inland sea remained. The geologists claimed that it had something to do with the giant earthquakes rearranging the edge of the tectonic plate known as the San Andreas Fault. Whatever— this lake, bay, or inland sea, remained as you can see. This same effect also caused most of Los Angeles to remain inundated as well as the bays you have recently seen in Lompoc and Santa Maria. It seems that the old San Andreas rift finally got its revenge on us poor Californians."

The "Five" had all moved to the ships side ports and their gasps now resembled a melancholy operatic chorus. Driscoll then recited the continuing litany of inundated cities now lost in the former heavily cultivated Valley. This was the valley that the "Oakies" and "Arkies" had descended upon during their escape from the "Dust Bowl" tragedy of the mid-1930's. It was the valley of John Steinbeck's novel, The Grapes of Wrath. Those migrant farmers had turned this, then barren, valley into one of the nations greatest vegetable, grain, and live-stock producing areas. Now, as they all witnessed, it was under many fathoms of glistening blue water which reflected back the images of the puffy white clouds soaring overhead.

"Sacramento, Stockton, Modesto, Merced, Fresno, Hanford, and Visalia… Should I continue?"

"That's enough Captain!"

Tom Brice certainly had heard enough when he held up his hand and proclaimed this.

"It's one thing to see this in a classroom presentation, far more disturbing to see it in bold reality. I can understand now why the 'Mile High City' has been chosen as the capital."

* * *

Shortly following the Lake San Joaquin shock, their ship headed across Nevada and the former location of the base where this great adventure had begun just two weeks, or a thousand years earlier. Then it was on across colorful Utah with its Brice Canyon and Zion National Park which could easily be seen as the pilot banked the aircraft, at Matt's request, in order to afford the passengers a proper view. Then it was smoothly up and over the western slope of the famous Rocky Mountains towards Grand Junction, Colorado. Here once again, they were surprised at the growth of this formerly small town located high in the Rockies. Grand Junction had spread out for miles as had the next town on their flight, 5700 foot high Glenwood Springs. These were now substantial cities, instead of the mountain villages that Tom Brice fondly remembered.

The soft background music that had been issuing from the overhead speakers suddenly changed to John Denver's famous rendition of his hit song, "Rocky Mountain High."

"That's appropriate considering where we are! I'm glad that old song has been kept in the modern inventories." Rob Carmody looked at Matt as he went on to say: "John Denver was very big in our time and he, like Elvis Presley, became more revered following his tragic death."

"The recordings of both of them are now considered to be important inclusions in our classical music inventory," responded Matt Driscoll.

While Denver's stirring performance continued, the passengers stared as if transfixed, out of the planes broad windows. They all could feel the emotion that the famous folk singer must have experienced when he looked up towards the high clouds through which they now sailed above the sparkling white peaks of those same Rocky Mountains. It was looking into these skies while lying on his back in the fields below, where John Denver, so long ago, penned the words to this now classic song.

As their aircraft slid in low over the eastern portion of the Mountains, it slowed perceptibly so that the passengers were able to see the rolling foothills just west of Denver. Denver's skyline shot up in front of them and stretched both north and south across the forward view-screen. The buildings were very tall and North America's second largest city was truly impressive.

As they swung in towards the edge of the city, Tom Brice noticed that the scrub covered plains at the base of the foothills ran abruptly up to the first line of green lawns next to the multi-storied buildings which all seemed to be bubbling with curved balconies.

"Where are the suburbs Matt? Where are the Westside suburbs?

"I'm sorry Tom. I guess we missed that part in the briefings."

"What part is that Matt?"

"There are no more suburbs. There are very few single-family homes—anywhere. Most housing is condominium styled. I guess the senator failed to mention that during her briefing. Owning and living in a single family house has been banned with the exception of farmers and people that work the land far from the cities. Most single family homes were destroyed by the disasters, none were rebuilt and most of those undamaged by the tsunamis and earth quakes were razed. Even some farmers commute to their work. There are some exceptions to all this, however they are rare."

"You mean this also is a world-wide phenomenon? Are you telling me that practically everyone on earth has to live in a God-damned apartment?"

"That's the way it is Colonel, however, on this trip you'll see that apartment living, or should I say 'Condo living,' is not exactly roughing it."

"Right Matt, sorry for the outburst. I'm just a little shocked to see what has happened to my old home town."

* * *

It was just after noon Mountain-Time on the 25$^{th}$ of April in the intriguing year 3030 when Matt Driscoll and the AG-1 crew disembarked at their predesignated landing area near the nations capitol in Denver, Colorado. They were all dressed in their new form fitting class A uniforms, which included well tailored jackets in Aerospace Service blue. These newly acquired jackets had their military rank insignia pinned on their epaulets. Even the enlisted sergeant stripes were embossed on pins that were attached to their epaulets. Rod Carmody had the five curved silver stripes below the star and the two silver chevrons above, denoting his rank of Senior Master Sergeant. Lilly and Norm's pins were similar with the exception of only a single chevron above the star, which was the symbol of a Master Sergeant. Remarkably, these insignia for senior non-commissioned officers in the Aerospace Service hadn't changed in all this time. Janet wore the gold oak leaves of a Major and Tom sported Lieutenant-Colonel's silver oak leaves pinned to his epaulets. These insignia also dated back more than a thousand years, as did Matt Driscoll's silver tracks of a Captain.

These neatly dressed and immaculately groomed service personnel simultaneously looked directly to their west, out across the expansive tarmac, and there unmistakably, loomed the imposing dome of the capitol of the United States. It seemed to them all as if this great symbolic building had been moved the 2000 miles from Washington D.C., completely intact. Following the crew members departure from the aircraft, they were once again on strict military protocol. When Tom Brice questioned Matt Driscoll about the capitol building, the captain responded:

"No Colonel Brice—the original was destroyed when the Potomac flooded along with everything else. The White House also has been reconstructed here. Luckily complete sets of plans came through the disasters. The original capitol, I've been told, was badly in need of repair just before the flood took care of that problem. They got most of the great masterpieces out to safety just in time, however they did loose some of the paintings and much of the fine furniture."

The "Five" once again felt the same feelings of awe that they had experienced in Washington prior to their life altering mission, as they climbed the massive stone steps that led to the east-side entrance. At the entrance they were greeted by a congressional committee headed by Senator Gina Krieger; then they were led into the vast Rotunda.

After entering the Rotunda, they were lined up at attention before a rostrum adorned with the seal of the President of the United States. With little fanfare, President of the United States David Rodriguez stepped up to the rostrum and proceeded to praise the five crew members. He was bronze skinned, tall, slender and handsome with his hair graying at the temples. He was dressed in a dark suit and a soft white turtle-neck shirt. At his throat was a small glittering medallion hanging from a deep blue ribbon, which seemed to replace the area previously occupied by the knot of a Twentieth Century necktie.

*That is exactly what presidents should have looked like in our time,* thought Lilly French as she studied her new Commander in Chief. She then smiled as she realized that such a description pretty well fit her President Obama, except for the graying temples.

*It's a matter of imagery... Distinguished looks evoke an air of competency, even when this may not be the case. Competency was the case with our Barach.*

The President then came forward, and with the help of Aerospace Service Chief General Kincaid, placed the Aerospace Service Distinguished Service Medal ribbons over the bowed heads; soon the attached spiked sunburst medallions sparkled at the throats of each of the five startled astronauts.

Tom Brice wondered about this as he returned the Presidential Salute:

*Why are we receiving so much attention? Hadn't other space and time travelers come through? Are we the only ones?*

Following the ceremony he quietly posed the same questions to Matt Driscoll.

"There have been others Colonel, and there are still some *out-there.* The difference is that you are the only ones to come from a time before the *disasters*. You few alone are our connection with the distant past."

"The *distant-past*, wow! You just aged us all Matt. Boy, I don't think *your* Lilly would appreciate that remark. By the way Matt, when there are no other people around, that is, other than our crew, I'm still Tom to you. I thought we had already discussed this, and you must be aware that the crew and I are on a first name basis."

"I'll try to remember that Tom, and I can see by your expression that you're not overly offended by the 'distant-past' remark. Also, thanks for giving me Lilly. *My Lilly*—that sounds pretty good to me."

The newly decorated crewmembers, with their Distinguished Service Medals hanging smartly around their necks, headed out of the west side of the Capitol Rotunda, led by Norm Johnson, the local boy when it came to the Capitol and other federal buildings. Spread out before them, in all its glory was the famous Capitol Mall. As they departed down the West side's wide marble steps, Norm remarked:

"They saved it all—look!"

Norm then pointed towards the west across the green expanse. In the distance they could see the replica of the Washington Monument as it pierced the sky in simple splendor. Directly beyond this giant obelisk they could see the left and right sides of the Lincoln Memorial peering out from behind the Washington Monument. The Jefferson Memorial loomed up as Norm shifted his gaze along the south-side of the Mall. Everything seemed to be in its proper place under the critical gaze of Sergeant Johnson. The Smithsonian Institute was also there on the south-side and the stately National Cathedral loomed up, to his right.

"It's all there and in the right position." Norm spoke out as if he were conducting a paid tour of the Capitol. "There's the White House—just down there to the right! I wonder if they have Japanese Cherry trees down by the lake alongside the Lincoln Memorial. I can't tell from here, in fact, I can't tell now if there even is a lake over there. I can see a replica of the magnificent Martin Luther King Memorial down there. I remember when they first built that back in Two Thousand and Seven. I was home on leave during some of the building. I even took some pictures of it. It was quite an event and they later had the formal dedication in the summer of Oh-eight."

Norm, and the others independently, decided not to bring up the word *replica* when discussing this scene with Matt or any of their friendly hosts. They correctly reasoned that that term might have a denigrating connotation, and obviously a massive effort and an enormous cost went into reproducing this spectacular scene. Norm reasoned that some of these memorials and magnificent buildings had been in his home town for only a century or two. Matt had explained to the crew that this Mall had been here for over six hundred years. Any remarks by the visitors that these structures were simply re-creations would now seem a little disingenuous.

This scene had a powerful affect on Norm. He thought of his home of Washington in his beloved District of Columbia, and he had difficulty getting it into his mind that it was all gone, as he viewed this great new Mall. He then lifted his gaze and there above the familiar scene were the unfamiliar, yet picturesque snow crowned Rocky Mountains jutting out of the horizon, easily viewed by all on the crystal clear morning. Here, reality came rushing back in. He was in Denver, at the foothills of the Rockies. Once again, and with some feeling of regret, he returned to the Fourth Millennium.

# CHAPTER FOURTEEN

That afternoon, the travelers were invited to stay at the military billets provided for them on the federal property a few miles east of downtown Denver. These condominiums were built on the land where Lowry Air Force Base had been located back in Tom Brice's youth.

Matt Driscoll escorted the "Five" into the multistoried apartment complex. The travelers had noticed the myriad of beautiful curved balconies surrounding the upper floors of the giant building. The other tall buildings in the area were also ringed with what seemed to be glass and brass railed balconies. The expansive lobby was beautifully decorated with what must have been contemporary décor for the time. Lilly noticed some rather muted, yet artistically precise paintings displayed around the lobby. In viewing these, Lilly wondered from what era, during their lost centuries of the previous millennium, had these works originated. There were two large used-brick fireplaces, one at either end of the main lobby. In front of each fireplace were thick comfortable looking couches. Some were occupied and a few of the tenants turned towards the new arrivals with questioning glances. Some wore military uniforms and many were in civilian clothes. They were informed that these were the family billets of married military officers and senior non-commissioned officers.

Even though the fires in the fireplaces burned brightly, Janet noticed that the temperature in the lounge seemed very comfortable. Following her question about the lack of noise from the air conditioning unit, Matt responded:

"Our 'air-conditioning' is somewhat different than what you folks are used to. In public rooms the temperature is maintained at seventy-three degrees Fahrenheit and the humidity is stabilized at forty-one percent. Bedrooms during sleep periods are normally set at sixty-eight degrees. Naturally these numbers can be changed, but they seldom are. It was decided a long time ago that these were the correct numbers for personal comfort. However, when the occupants get to a certain age, normally around one hundred, their metabolism slows and they seem to prefer warmer temperatures. In the common-rooms, like these, the temperatures are set as I described."

Rob looked about for air-registers or ducts. There weren't any visible and he recalled the same phenomenon back at their rooms in the Operations Building at Vandenberg.

Against the far wall of the high ceiling room was a bank of elevators doors. There also was an unmanned desk near the elevators and Matt went quickly over to it. He punched a couple of numbers into a rather benign looking computer and out of a slot popped three key cards. He then waved his little group forward and they all headed for the elevators.

Just before entering the elevators Janet Hulse asked: "Where are the shops, the beauty parlors? Where are the stores?"

Janet's questions were not aimed at any one individual; they were simply a continuing inquisitive search for what was going on. Naturally, Matt immediately responded:

"They're right below us Janet. You see, down that wide hall to your right. There's the stairwell railing and there are wide stairs going down to the lower floors. Of course the elevators go down there as well. All the shops are down there on the lower two floors with a sub-basement below them. The sub-basement handles all the utilities and supply inputs for this building. Each of those lower floors have twelve foot high ceilings. As well as the shops, there are some business offices down there. As you will soon see, other offices are in the private condominiums above. I'll point these out to you when I show you where you'll be staying during your leave. By the way, this building is known as The Stapleton Arms."

"Stapleton—that was the name of the Denver Airport when I was a boy," remarked Tom Brice.

"It seems that everything the citizens will need are right here in these buildings."

"That's right Tom—certainly the necessities for a comfortable life are all hear. Even the 'Pre-schools' and 'Elementary schools' that we spoke of, are here in these buildings. These schools normally occupy the second and third floors. We don't want the young students going to class totally under artificial light if we can avoid it. There are even 'Middle' and 'High schools' in some of these residential buildings. These really are very large buildings. Also they are constructed from building materials that were not available in your time. The main structures such as this building are expected to last a thousand years without major structural renovation. I believe that this particular block of condominiums is approximately three hundred years old."

"Whoa—they look like they're brand new. Very impressive, now what about churches? Are they also found in these buildings?"

Norm asked this while studying a well equipped children's playground and colorful garden beyond one of the lobby's massive glass walls.

"Most of our churches are in the downtown part of our cities, Norm. That is the case here in Denver."

Tom Brice then pointed down the wide stairwell that Matt had shown them, and said: "These then are the locations of small private businesses in this era—right Matt?"

"That's only partly so Tom. You see, there really aren't any small privately owned businesses anymore. In fact, there are no privately owned businesses large or small. These are all franchise outlets controlled by The Business Manage…"

"Yes—of course. The Business Management Division of the United Nations in Bern, Switzerland."

"That's it Tom. The prices for goods and services offered by these stores are regulated for only a small margin of profits. Naturally, there is enough to pay the 'help' along with space rent, utilities and clerical costs. The space rent goes to the local governing body. With the five percent sales tax going to the different levels of government, that's it in pricing. No fifty or one hundred percent markups. There are no excessive profits, therefore the established price for goods and services, is low and enduring."

"Is there a 'Downtown' shopping area as well? Are there shopping malls or something like those nice stores near the park back in Santa Maria?"

"Yes Lilly. All of our large cities have fine shopping areas as well as galleries, theaters, museums and the like. The difference is that these and the larger downtown stores are still franchised. The large department stores, for example, do sell a wide assortment of products. These are still controlled from Bern. Along with this pricing, our styles are controlled."

"Price control I can live with Matt, but style…? I'll never get used to style being controlled by bureaucrats—that sounds awful!"

"Wait a second sweetheart… The bureaucrats don't establish styles, the particular industries involved do. The bureaucrats control the prices and distribution, sometimes they do step in to prevent a breakdown of product design."

"That's still a form of censorship Mathias Darling. That's still 'Big Brother' reaching in—way in."

"Well—I guess it is my lovely lady, but that's the way the whole thing works…"

* * *

Prior to heading out to Denver, Matt had booked these apartments. He knew that these were typical of the condominiums that now housed a majority of the human race. It was here that he could more easily answer their personal questions concerning life-styles and "Life Leases," as well as acceptable living conditions in the modern world. The little rooms back at Vandenberg's Operations Building were not exactly good examples.

Matt tried his card-key at the first condo door, then waived them all inside.

When the newly decorated crew members were shown their rooms, they began to realize what was referred to as the new "*Condo*" standard of living, actually meant. They weren't rooms at all, but rather lavish apartments.

"These units are typical of single or double occupancy condominiums now used throughout the world. However, many of the beautiful old stone homes from Europe and the Eastern United States still survive from your time and are still in use today. Some of these buildings were close to a thousand years old when you all left. They have been restructured and refurbished and are very much sought after. Most of these fit into the size limitations that I'm about to discuss with you. Many of these fine old mansions that exceeded the Bern limitations were divided into two or more condominiums. We haven't taken down these old gems of the past. One reason that they are considered special is that many of these are the only ancient buildings that survived the great earthquakes and floods."

Matt had a touch of pride in his voice as he waived his hand indicating the expanse of the living room.

"All three units, you'll find, are similar in size and appointments, yet not identical."

"Three units?" remarked a questioning Rob.

Matt turned to Rob and Norm and explained:

"You two will share this one for the thirty days. I take it that this is okay with you sergeants seeing that you shared a space ship for a thousand years."

"Five days Matt, just five days—but of course it's alright," remarked a smiling Rob Carmody, as Norm nodded, adding his approval.

"The government only authorized three units, however seeing that the Aerospace Service is paying for them, we better not complain. This unit has two single beds in the bedroom, so it shouldn't be that great a hardship. I guess the rest of us will have to share as well. This means that Tom and Janet will be in the unit next door and Lilly and I will have to suffer through in the unit down the hall. I've already discussed this with Tom and Janet and of course with Lilly. We, however, will have to put up with another great hardship in these other two units. Each of the other single bedrooms, sadly, are only equipped with a rather luxurious queen sized bed."

"How devastating! You mean Tom and Janet are going to share one unit and you and Lilly the other. We all know about Tom and Janet and I suspected something like this with you and Lilly, but I'm still a little surprised. Now, just how do you know that the queen sized beds are so luxurious?" responded a grinning Rob Carmody.

"That's what the automated recording said when I booked these rooms. I was just fooling about the government only authorizing three units. That's all I requested after discussing it with Lilly. Things are different here in many ways Rob. Actually co-habitation prior to marriage is not just tolerated but practically required. Something to do with the divorce rates of earlier eras."

"Prior to marriage... Are you and Lilly planning to get married along with Tom and Janet?"

Rob's question hung before them all on the still clear air of the plush apartment.

Matt turned towards the rather shocked, very pretty red-haired master sergeant.

"I 'm not sure Rob... What's your answer Lilly? You know I'm crazy about you."

Matt suddenly dropped to one knee and looked up into the blushing face of his intended.

"I love you Lilly—I mean I *really* love you... Will you marry me?"

Lilly then dropped to her knees on the soft carpet, grabbed her handsome young man around the neck and planted a big kiss on his mouth.

"I didn't her a yes yet!" exclaimed Tom. "Where's the yes?"

Lilly mumbled something that was barely audible without breaking the kiss, and Tom quickly responded:

"That should suffice! It's now official!"

They all laughed at this and after regaining his feet and his equilibrium, Matt now sporting a broad grin, lifted his Lilly to her feet. The two caught their breath before they tumbled happily into the nearby couch. After a few minutes of hugs and congratulations all around, Matt once again took over and led the cheerful little group on a tour of the apartment. The entrance into the apartment had seemed somewhat formal to the crew, with its colorful ceramic tiled flooring that stretched to the edge of the deeply carpeted living room, and its ten foot high ceiling. From the crown molding edged ceiling hung an attractive chandelier that still allowed a seven and one half foot clearance, well above the tallest of occupants, including "Moderns."

Matt pointed to the ceiling in the living room and stated:

"The norm of eight foot ceilings from your time has given way to ten foot ceilings. It's the volume in an apartment, as well as the square footage, that makes it desirable. This has become part of the International Building Code."

"International Building Code,?" questioned Tom. "And, by the way, ten foot ceilings were becoming the norm when we left."

"Sorry about that Tom. I'm sure there will be other historical inaccuracies made by me during our conversations. Anyway, yes we have an International Building Code administered from Bern, Switzerland. The United Nations you understand."

"The United Nations seems to have one hell of a lot more power and authority than they did in our time!" responded the Colonel.

"I believe that they do. All living or sitting rooms must be a least twenty feet long in one dimension and at least fifteen feet wide in the other. No bedrooms can have dimensions of less than twelve feet in either length or width. Therefore, twelve by twelve is the smallest a bedroom can be, not counting walk-in closet space for the master bedroom. All condominium apartments must have at least one twelve by ten foot office space in addition to the bedrooms. All common or 'party' walls are soundproofed. Even these interior walls are insulated to such a degree that they are virtually soundproof. Most clerical work is done at home now and the virtual office becomes a real office in that one holographic wall opens up into a formal office or another home based office, depending on the wishes of the occupant. Meetings and interviews can be conducted in these rooms and the effect, of course, is at least a twelve by twenty foot long office visit. Saves a great deal on transportation and company operational cost."

"Good idea—makes sense."

Tom said this and the rest agreed.

The kitchen was rather small and was separated from the dining area by an island, or more accurately, a low peninsula. In the dining area a wooden dining table with six padded chairs sat stoically below a fine multi-bulb chandelier. The kitchen appointments were very impressive and equally confusing to the travelers.

"I'll have to go through the kitchen with you all after I finish showing you the rest of the apartment. The appliances are different as are many of the cooking utensils. Let's all sit down at this dining table, there are a few more things about these universal apartments that I want to tell you about."

As they sat down Rob asked:

"What's the square footage of this unit Matt?"

"This particular unit is right at thirteen hundred square feet, which is typical of one bedroom units. This is also the minimum square footage allowed in Life Leases. Two bedroom units average around sixteen hundred square feet. Three bedrooms are normally limited to nineteen hundred."

Tom looked at Matt and said:

"That would make a four bedroom unit about twenty-two hundred square feet, or should I say limited to twenty-two hundred— right?"

"There are no four bedroom units in level one Tom. Remember the discussion about birth and population controls? The only four bedroom units are allowed to provide a single guest room for the more successful. One has to apply for that privilege and it depends on the owner's profession and position. Normally no more than two children per family—remember Sir? However, if a couple was given special permission for a third child they also would be allowed a fourth bedroom. That permission wouldn't be given to a family qualified at level one. Therefore these units are limited to nineteen hundred square feet, as I mentioned."

"Yes, I see Matt. Then it takes a couple qualified for what, a higher level status to get the extra bedroom? Or is nineteen hundred square feet the absolute limit, as directed by our friends at the United Nations?"

"Not quite Tom. As I mentioned, there are some incentives for those whom excel in the areas of medicine, business, sports or *the arts* or any acceptable profession, including senior military ranks. There are two more levels of apartment luxury that is determined by size and appointments. The second level allows sixteen hundred square feet for a one bedroom, two thousand feet for a two bedroom, twenty-four hundred for the three, and those special allowed four bedroom units max out at twenty-eight hundred square feet."

"What about the third level?" asked Janet. "How about level three for the rich and successful—yet not ostentatious?"

This again brought a laugh from all including Matt, who was still a little high on Lilly's passionate acceptance of his proposal.

This, of course is the ultimate, Janet. The one bedroom units for the most successful are two thousand square feet and the balconies are larger and the ten foot high ceilings have indirect lighted, oval shaped, artistically decorated, fourteen inch higher 'trays,' or center ceiling extensions. They also have a few other little architectural nuances. The two bedroom units measure twenty-five hundred square feet, the threes are three thousand and the fours top out at thirty-five hundred square feet. That's it… That's the ultimate—thirty-five hundred. Of course these numbers vary, only slightly, very slightly. You don't want to be caught with thirty-six hundred square feet of indoor living space."

"I guess that would be looked upon as extremely pretentious!" quipped Janet who had been raised in a much larger home. "Just what would be the penalty for such anti-social behavior?"

"The builder or contractor involved in such a building code breach would be admonished and if the practice continued, reprogramming would be a possibility. The same is true for those individuals who ordered such extensions. Also, such violations would require a retrofit if they had been completed."

"Matt my boy… Once an individual has reached that upper level of condominium living, what then are their incentives to reach further—strive harder?"

Tom felt that he knew what the answer to this question would be before he asked it. However, he wanted to see if he was right and wanted to hear it articulated by the bright young officer.

"Pride Tom—pride and the welfare of others. Pride and the 'common good.' These are real powerful emotions Sir, and we have found that we all have them lurking somewhere in the deep recesses of our brain. We all have them hidden away deep in our personal 'hard-drives.' We have finally discovered that human's are basically good, even us male members of society. All we needed was to get far enough away from that survival based fury that was necessary in the 'cave-man' years, which, as you can see, we've finally stepped beyond. That trait is no longer required and no longer wanted. We truly are a more compassionate people now and I'm certain that this applies to you all. We finally have become *ladies and gentlemen*!"

"Thank you Matt. That is what I thought your answer would be, however, I didn't expect such an articulate response. Well said young man, and congratulations on that other thing! You two will make a fine couple."

This drew a unified response and once again, congratulations all around.

By now the group had been led out to the broad balcony, and the view was impressive. Denver had grown by a factor of eight since Tom had left. Even though the apartment buildings were spaced some distance apart, the extreme height of the forty story buildings brought back memories of New York for Lilly.

While on the balcony, Matt had everyone sit down on the attractive weather proof chairs that surrounded a small glass top table. He stood by the railing and addressed them as if he were about to present a formal lecture:

"When Major Hansen briefed you on the disasters of the late Twenty First and early Twenty-Second Centuries, he omitted another rather significant natural phenomenon that occurred during your little trip. He figured that you had received enough emotional trauma at that time and I requested that he not discuss the subject of 'Magnetic Pole Reversal.' I told him before the briefing that we would go over this event at a later date. That later date is now."

"Holy mackerel… More disasters?"

"Not quite so serious Norm. It seems that we were better prepared for this one. We had sufficient warning, due to our studies of Solar Flares. Our "ACE-Four" satellite, permanently located between us and the sun, gave us the necessary lead time to make some preparations."

"I knew something about this before we left Matt."

"I'm sure you did Tom and especially you Janet. By the time you folks left regular compass readings were becoming flawed, especially when flying over the South Atlantic and up there in the 'Bermuda Triangle' of the mid-Atlantic."

"That's right Matt," replied Janet. "The compass readings for magnetic North had to constantly be recalibrated, and in those two areas a magnetic 'hot-spot' had developed. Luckily, when we went to our global positioning satellites, or GPS, our magnetic compasses were no longer required."

"That's it Janet. That's one of the reasons that all of our air borne activities rely on GPS as well as Anti-Grav. This has long been a requirement in all aircraft. Anyway, the poles finally switched polarity rapidly from Twenty-Four Thirteen through Fifteen. As I mentioned, we saw it coming and were able to recalibrate everything shortly afterward. However, there was an extended period of disruption, and there was a problem with the increase in the penetration of the sun's radiation.

Other dangerous forms of deep-space radiation swept in, during this period of change. There was an increase in deadly skin cancers despite the warnings concerning exposure to direct sun light.

"We have since cured all cancers and the radiation penetrations have returned to the levels enjoyed back in the Nineteenth Century. The people of that reverse-polar time, recorded the magnificent solar flares that could be seen world-wide. I believe you folks referred to them as 'Aurora Borealis' and they could only be seen near the Artic Circle during your time. You all, I believe, are aware that the earth's magnetic field shielded us from most of this harmful radiation? You know, the 'Solar Winds.'"

"How long was this period of disruption, as you put? How long did the sun's radiation pose an extreme threat, before the earth's magnetism once again strengthened enough to protected us? Is it the Spring of the year, or are we headed for winter— Matt?"

"April is now in the Fall, and the weakening of the field started early in the Twentieth Century Rob. It didn't become critical until the middle of the Twenty-First. Just a few decades after your departure, I believe. Your little time-jump came at a very propitious time in human history. It only returned to its present strength about two hundred years ago. Now, remember my friends, if you wish to use a compass, the needle currently points to the South Magnetic Pole."

Matt Driscoll now led his little group back into the apartment and entered the well appointed, yet limited sized "entertainment room" which was located on the left side of the open entrée area. This room had a high quality sectional sofa set with accompanying coffee and end-tables located at its far side. The entertainment room, being only the prescribed twelve feet long and twelve feet wide, seemed rather small to be considered an entertainment or family-room area. Behind the large sofa was a doorway, which Matt explained led to the single bedroom. Matt asked his guests to make themselves comfortable on the four cushion couch as he and Lilly sat in the adjacent, aptly named, love-seat. Spread across the far wall was a beautiful color-line mural illustrating a Mediterranean Villa by that famous sea.

Lilly remarked about its quality, however she also asked why there was no other furniture on that side of the room.

"Is this same mural used in every apartment? I like it—but is this the only choice Matt?"

"No sweetheart, but there are only twenty. Now I'll show you why there isn't any furniture on that side of the room."

"Well, twenty, that should certainly be enough variety with the restricted tastes of you *moderns*." Lilly offered this with a good natured dig into Matt's ribs.

Matt picked up a conveniently placed remote-control and the far wall of their small entertainment room suddenly blossomed into a vast three dimensional window on the world. They all were now sitting on comfortable cushions looking out onto the terraced hills of Southern China. It was no longer a static line mural of a Mediterranean Villa. They were in China, watching an old documentary of peasant workers in their ancient rice fields. Although they had recently been exposed to very graphic holographic presentations, something seemed different about this even more thrilling presentation. Matt then clicked a button and they were flying through the clouds along side of picturesque Mount Kilimanjaro on the continent of Africa. The immediate and unanimous expletive was, "Wow!"

Certainly this magnificent surround sound system was superior to the holographic presentations of the Vandenberg Control Center offices, yet there was something else. It was subtle, however there was simultaneous recognition among the five.

"My God !— We can smell the air in there, I can almost feel what's out there!"

Toms exclamations were mirrored by the rest of his surprised crew-members.

"They tried something like this back in our time," said Rob Carmody.

"They tried it, yet it never caught on, and it certainly wasn't as technically sophisticated as this. They called those presentations 'Smellies.'"

Matt turned down the sound on the screen so that he could explain.

"Those didn't catch on Rob, because they actually piped different fragrances into the theaters that were involved. The smells could not be changed instantly like these, and different people had different reactions to the scents. Often negative reactions, I might add."

Matt continued his entertaining presentation by saying:

"You are not experiencing chemical fragrances. Instead it is various super-sonic wave lengths that stimulate the olfactory senses in the brain. This is why the sensations changed abruptly as I changed the scene. Naturally, we have thousands of these programs from all over the planet and the solar-system as well. We also have thousands of motion pictures formatted for these personal holographic systems including many computer regenerated offerings from your era."

Matt stood up after showing approximately ten minutes of these dramatic scenes to his appreciative audience, and added: "This has actually cut down on one's desire for travel. Don't miss-understand me here when I say it has cut down travel. It certainly hasn't cut out everyone's desire to explore new areas. We all still desire the interactions with others throughout the world, and 'being there' still beats the holographs. Now I'll put up a rather interesting landing on Mars and a brief exploration of our base there."

# CHAPTER FIFTEEN

THE CREW REALLY ENJOYED the holographic presentations, not only the landing on Mars but everything that Matt showed. He now steered them back into the kitchen and it was time for them to be brought up to speed concerning the preparation of food in this new millennium. First, Matt discussed the process of getting food into the apartment without the use of individually owned vehicles. Matt pulled what looked to be a multi-paged menu from between two of the counter level cabinets.

"Here it is guys! If it ain't in here we ain't got it. If we ain't got it—you don't get it."

"You mean this is all there is?" remarked Lilly as she took the offered menu from Matt's hand.

"Actually, there's quite a lot in there Lilly. There are thirty-six pages of offerings."

"My God! They're TV Dinners!" exclaimed his startled red-haired girl friend.

"Well, wait a minute sweetheart. I wouldn't use a derogatory term in discussing the food that your going to be eating for the rest of your life. I'm guessing that *T V Dinners* is derogatory by the tone of your voice. Actually, I hadn't heard that term used before your arrival."

"I'm sorry Matt Darling, I guess these are what we all have been eating ever since we arrived, and I must admit that they are pretty damned good."

"Anyway," Matt continued: "You place your order through this device and the meals will come up through the chute into this cabinet.

Most people order up a weeks supply of meals at one time, and store them in this freezer here."

With this, Matt moved to his left and opened the wooden cabinet door which revealed a multi shelved freezer. Naturally, it was empty. He then turned back and raised the lid on an innocuous cabinet which was located next to what looked like a stack of two medium sized microwave ovens. The colorful menu had been hiding between these appliances.

"There are two ovens so that different dinner requirements for two can be warmed simultaneously. Also, there is a warming oven here for when there are more than two for a meal. Before one orders them up, these meals are stored in the 'freezer-room' of the basement in this and all other living quarter complexes."

"Please don't say it again Matt, not *world-wide* ?"

Matt shook his head in the affirmative to Norm's question.

"You mean everyone in *your* wide world has the same taste. Is that it Matt, we all are going to eat the same food?"

Norm Johnson was quite serious with this response.

"Yes Norm, and remember that it is your wide world as well. I believe that you'll find quite an extensive variety of breakfast meals, lunch meals and dinner choices. These, along with a variety of snacks and Hors d'Oeuvres, as well as beers, wines, and liquor, fill out these thirty-six pages. No space consuming pictures on that menu, just the listings. These are also listed on the small screen here above the cabinet, however, this also includes a picture of the offerings."

With this, Matt punched a button and then scrolled the computer screen. He then turned towards a tall cabinet in matching wood finish with the rest of the kitchen, and asked Lilly to open the pair of doors. It was the refrigerator and it also was empty except for a complementary bottle of wine and a two liter bottle of water. The refrigerators and freezers were separate appliances.

"I'm certain that you folks can fill this up during your thirty day stay. Remember, however, we'll be eating out a lot, so please don't over indulge on your computer food requests."

"What about brand-names Matt? What about advertising? Do we get a choice?

"Only the best and most efficient companies survived. This was determined in Bern." Matt turned towards Tom in answering his questions:

"Competition as you knew it is gone now Tom. Of course there are many giant farm cooperatives throughout the world as well as food processing companies, however their distribution areas are determined by the United Nations. We don't have the inefficiency of competing corporations. If you noticed during our travels, there aren't any billboards exclaiming the superiority of their products while blocking the scenic beauty that surrounds us. We don't have our evening entertainment interrupted by constant and irritating commercials, that I noticed in my studies of your era, yet the officials at Bern are able to control costs and insure a high level of quality. It's really pay television. These are some of the controls that the people at the UN are paid to insure for the benefit of all of us."

"What about all the other products Matt? It's true—I haven't seen or heard any advertising since we've been here. Do the people in Bern, Switzerland, control everything?"

"Just about Rob, they determine just what is the best in every field and of course in every climate and these are the products allowed. You'll get computer readouts on all of these. And yes, they control taste and content, which had gotten way out of control earlier."

"That certainly gives the people at the United Nations extraordinary powers." Rob Carmody then asked their host: "How do you keep these beauraucrats from miss-using their powers—or do you?"

"Working at the UN is a great honor Rob. But, we still have a good deal of control over these people, and their actions. The actions of that body in general, are quite transparent. There is a steady flow of data concerning their procurement practices and all other aspects of their actions, as well. They can be removed for inefficiency or fraud quite easily. However, think of this... Why would any of these United Nations employees risk their reputation to try to make more money. Their lifestyles wouldn't change one iota. The individuals there that control procurement, and everything else for that matter, are already living at the maximum standard of living allowed. What in the world would be their motivation to do something illegal. That my friends is true throughout the entire world now. This is the biggest reason for the lack of monetary based crime. As you all stand here in this apartment, you're looking at the standard of living of the least of us. Why would anyone risk being *reprogrammed*—because of this?"

Tom Brice merely shook his head slowly and said nothing.

Matt then walked around the small kitchen showing some of the utensils, indicating where the table-ware was located and pointing out the trash disposal unit. There was a fine stainless double kitchen sink with garbage disposal and a dishwasher to round out the appliances.

"Although the dinners come in plastic trays, we still use china-ware and of course glasses and cutlery, hence the dishwasher. We're not Neanderthal's my friends—we still appreciate some of the finer things of life."

Lilly looked at Matt and smiled:

"I'm well aware of that sweetheart. Now let me get this straight. This is the smallest unit and yet it has an entrée, a living room, an office, an entertainment room a bedroom, and a small dining room along with this kitchen. What about bathrooms, Mathias? "

"Of course, my love. These small units have a master bath I'll show you in a few minutes. They're equipped with two sinks, a separate shower along with a Jacuzzi style tub and the toilet. There's also a separate lavatory for guests. Now don't forget the deck, My Dear, when listing this unit's attributes."

"Your right Matt when you say that these units really are plush!"

Tom Brice seemed very much impressed when he stated this and the others whole heartedly agreed. However, Tom was far more apprehensive about so much power going to the United Nations. His memory was too fresh when he thought about the corruption and scandals concerned with that organization when it was located in New York City.

Matt now turned to what resembled a broom closet door and started to opened it.

"This my friends is probably the most interesting item in this apartment."

He swung the door open, and staring out at them all was an approximately five foot tall, slender, beige colored robot. There was no light coming from its glassy eyes, only a small red light shone from the center of its forehead, indicating that it was in the re-charge mode. Matt addressed the human shaped robot and the red light flicked off. The machine's pale green eyes lit up, and it stepped out of the closet and clearly said:

"May I be of some assistance?"

The crew members were stunned by this, even though Tom and Rob had expected to eventually see some fancy robotics, after being informed about their extreme 'time-jump.' Even they were startled by the life-like appearance of this machine. 'DAR' was dressed in light blue coveralls and it had a small tool belt at it's waist. On the robot's chest was the colorful logo of The Stapleton Arms.

Matt then pointed to Rob and Norm as he addressed the robot:

"DAR—these are Sergeants Carmody and Johnson. They will be your controllers for the next thirty days."

Matt then turned to Rob and said:

"Go ahead Rob, ask DAR if it would now please check the unit for dust and dirt." Matt explained that he was able to give the initial orders because it was he who had the apartment's card-key.

Rob gave the instructions and the machine first reached back into the closet for a small hand-held vacuum unit, an then it briskly stepped off towards the apartments entrée. As soon as the robot was out of sight, the questions came:

"It looks like a rather frail small person. Is it frail? It has a very bland face, nothing there you could warm up to. Does it have any feelings Matt?"

"No Lilly, not at all frail—no emotional feelings. It's a machine and that's why we refer to it, as 'It.' They didn't want to give these things too much personality, that's why that plain emotionless expression. Remember what you all were told during your briefings. These are simply machines, just elaborate tools. When they are privately owned, their owners normally provide more attractive clothing for the little rascals."

"How did you know its name Matt? Are they all named DAR?"

"Another acronym, Tom. DAR stands for Domestic Assistance Robot. These names are normally changed when people acquire their own personal unit. However, in rental units they all go by 'DAR.' There are other robot acronyms such as LAR for Land Assistance Robot. Those robots are outside workers such as farm and ranch help, and they are larger. Then there's MAR for Manufacturing Assistance Robot, which includes non-humanoid industrial robots.

"Also, and this is quite important, we have GAR for General Assistance Robot. Naturally, people working with these more advanced machines give them specific and personal names not just numbers in order to keep them straight. These individual names are normally embroidered on their clothing. The GAR series robots are the most life-like. They have very human facial features and although there are only a couple of dozen facial patterns, both male and female, they're not easy to spot as robots, at a distance. Also, these GAR robots dress in contemporary civilian clothes; they are even taller than the LAR series, and they are referred to according to their obvious gender designs. They blend in quite well with the rest of us, which was the plan."

"How much can they do Matt? Just how adroit are these things?"

"Let's put it this way Norm, their manual dexterity is similar to a humans. Did you notice how life-like DAR's hands were. These things can do just about anything necessary to work a domestic household, or if they are out in the other professions, they can perform equally well. We're extremely proud of these things, and I must admit that we are also quite dependent on them as well. They prepare our meals, which of course is merely removing the dinners from the freezer or refrigerator, placing them in the micro-wave oven and setting the time and temperature, and then serving them to us at the dining table, or on the patio, or...

"They can make our beds, clean the apartment and do our clothes washing. They also answer the door and escort in invited guests. One must program who's invited for they won't let uninvited individuals in—security you understand. There's a spring-steel skeleton under that smooth beige skin, so when it comes to security, they are capable."

"I thought that you didn't need security anymore Matt. You know—no crime an all?"

"We really don't Janet, Maybe it's just a hangover from the past, yet you never know who will show up at your door. Remember—passion is still with us."

Lilly subtly nodded her head in the affirmative.

"These robots are sort of a psychological security blanket, I guess. However, everyone likes it this way. When renters such as we, first open up one of these apartments, they have to do what I just did—that is activate DAR. From now on, DAR here, will answer your door when you return from wherever, and politely ask what it can do for your comfort. We also have robots in the military and they are used to perform particularly hazardous tasks. All these robots are capable of communicating with each other in a non-verbal way. This is necessary when they are working in groups or teams, or, I might add, in military situations. These non-verbal communications are similar to cellular phone contacts that we still use. The difference is that they are nearly instantaneous non-verbal strings of digital codes that spark silently through the atmosphere. Something to do with 'Singularity' I've been told."

"My God… You're not a robot—are you Matt. I'm not in love with a damned robot, or am I Mathias?"

"Not funny Lilly. You certainly know better than that. While on this fascinating subject—robots do not have sex organs. That's a real 'no no,' and if any of them were used in this manner, and it was discovered, there owners would probably face *re-programming."*

"Just a minute Matt," Tom softly interjected. Can humans monitor those strings of digital communications between robots?"

"It takes specialized equipment Tom, however, we don't find this necessary seeing that we have programmed them to obey us. You shouldn't find a robot giving orders to a human, only to each other. The whole thing is quite safe. Remember we discussed this subject back at Vandenberg."

Soon, DAR returned to the kitchen and stood in front of his cabinet.

"Are there any further request, Sir?" DAR's voice was soft, pleasant and easy to understand.

"Not now—thank you DAR," came Rob's reply as directed by Matt. The robot remained standing in front of the cabinet and the soft light in its soft green eyes blinked out.

"When I give it the order, it will enter the cabinet and plug in its own charging unit. I should say when you, either of you, Rob, Norm, give it the orders for the rest of our leave, it will respond."

*   *   *

Following their initial tour of the 'level-one' apartment, Matt left Norm, Rob and their DAR in that unit so they could unpack and decide who would sleep where.

"We'll be back for you guys in a couple of hours and then we'll all go downstairs and test the cuisine in this mausoleum."

Matt then led Janet and Tom to their assigned condo which was located next door to Norm and Rob's unit. He then presented Tom with their card-key, then proceeded down the hall to his and Lilly's temporary home. All three units were on the same floor which made it convenient for their many anticipated get-togethers.

At seven that evening the crew assembled in the rather plush basement restaurant. It was Chaison's.

"This isn't really Chaison's," remarked Janet.

"It's a clone Matt. It's one of your damned clones, isn't it? Or, should I say *franchises…?"*

"Yes Jan… Let's not be critical until we've had our dinner. Then you may all bombard me with your criticisms."

The dinner proved to be a delight and Janet apologized to Matt for her remarks about 'clones' and 'franchises.'

Tom then asked Matt if their meals had also come from the thirty-six page menu that they had seen in the apartment.

"No Tom… This is where your meals are cooked from scratch. This, I guess, is where our meals come close to the quality of the meals from your era. These restaurants, and there are twenty-one different chains world-wide, are allowed to order their raw ingredients pre-prepared. These restaurants actually heir 'Chefs,' which, I might add, is very honored profession."

"It was in our time as well Matt, and the food here really is great!"

Rob's enthusiastic approval was seconded by all.

"This is one of the areas that extra income can be an incentive. These dinners are not cheap. But, again, who is going to risk criminal charges for a few extra meals out at one of these fine restaurants?"

Matt said this as he picked up the bill, glanced at it, and then placed it along with his government debit card into the little black plastic tray.

"The check is two hundred and forty Megas for the six of us—but who's counting? Our beloved Aerospace Service is paying for this one."

"Me… I will…! I'll risk criminal charges, I'll go to jail for another meal like this one. It may well be the best dinner I've ever had!"

Norm said this with a big grin as Rob soberly added:

"He's not kidding!"

"What about a 'Tip' Matt?"

Lilly picked up the check from the tray and repeated: "Do you add the Tip to this check? What's the normal percentage for Tips?"

"What… What are you talking about sweetheart. What the devil is a *Tip*?'

"You jest… You don't give gratuities to those who wait on you, or carry your luggage, or cut your hair, or…?"

"They're paid properly for this kind of work and many of these tasks are performed by robots. What's a robot going to do with a gratuity? I'm sorry darling—I guess you didn't notice; that was a robot that just waited on our table."

"Whoa!" came the chorus from the startled space travelers.

"That was no DAR," added Lilly.

"I'm sorry folks. I thought that I mentioned that some of these robots, such as that particular GAR, have been designed to look lifelike, and behave like humans."

"She was beautiful," was Rob's immediate response to this.

"She was an excellent waitress and very friendly—I might add."

Lilly thought about this for a moment and then said:

"She looked a lot like that young woman back at the Vandenberg Coffee Shop. My God… I was getting jealous of a God damned robot. She, or should I say 'It,' even posed for me so I could take its picture. Matt, you don't know what kind of a dope your getting hooked up with."

"Your far from a dope, Darling. It's not easy to tell some of these GAR robots from humans. We 'Moderns' are used to them and it's easier for us to identify them, but your reaction only means that we've done a good job in creating them. Thanks for the compliment my beautiful girl. None of them are, or ever will be as pretty as you."

* * *

While rapidly ascending in the elevator towards their twelfth floor apartments, Matt softly interjected:

"Breakfast at Lilly and my place. Seven AM—don't be late. Oh, I almost forgot this little insignificant item. Tomorrow nights dinner is at the 'White House' so please don't make any other plans for tomorrow evening. I believe that it will be followed by a concert at the Sergei Rachmaninov Concert Hall, featuring the arias of Joe Green and Jack Pucci."

"Wow—another one of your jokes Matt?"

"I'm afraid not Tom… You'll just have to suffer through it."

"Joe Green and Jack Pucci, very funny Matt. My favorite operatic composers of all time. Of course guys, you realize that he's referring to Giuseppe Verdi and Giacomo Puccini. My God, what will I wear? What will we all wear? We probably can't find the proper clothes, especially on a Sunday."

"Hold on sweetheart… We've been requested to attend this rather gala affair in uniform. Our class A's should be fine Lilly, and all of you should wear your newly acquired Distinguished Service Medals at the throat of your white dress shirts."

"Sounds great Matt, maybe they'll throw in an Irish Ballad or two."

"I wouldn't doubt it Rob—I think something like that really is in the works."

Janet then looked up at their tall young sponsor and said:

"I really love Grand Opera, along with Lilly here. Damn… Maybe we really are celebrities— I only hope I can look the part."

"If anyone here looks the part, it's you Janet. You'll knock ém dead!"

"I'll second that Matt," said a grinning Tom Brice.

As Matt opened the door to their floor, and just before stepping out onto the thickly carpeted hall, Norm looked at Matt wistfully, then added:

"Boy, this really is great. Dinner with the President at the White House. God, I wish my mother was here to know about this. I sure wish both Mom and Dad were here to know about this one Matt. It would have made them so happy. They really would have been proud of me."

"They are proud of you Norm. There's not the slightest doubt in my mind… They know…"

# CHAPTER SIXTEEN

THE MORNING GET-TOGETHER FOR the now "Six" comrades, was filled with delightful conversation and anticipation concerning the coming evening event at the White House. It was determined by the two young ladies that they would spend the afternoon in downtown Denver doing what young ladies do, *Shopping* and getting their hair *Done.*

"It's Sunday," Lilly reminded her friends.

"Matt Dear, please check and see if any of the downtown Beauty Parlors are open, and what about transportation?"

"They all are Darling, I've already checked. Now, I'll have to show you two where the 'Light-Rail' stop is and which one you should take. You'll be heading down Colfax Avenue to Sixteenth Street. Most of the stores and shops are in that area. I know that you'll be looking for some formal clothes while you're downtown, however, remember what I said. The President specifically requested that we *all* show up in uniform. We guys will be going to a ball game at Mile High Stadium this afternoon. You young ladies are certainly welcome to come to the game with us, if you want?"

Matt announced this while studying the reactions of his tall, red-haired, vivacious, *fiancé.* Her reaction, along with her close friend Janet's, was obvious. Shopping in downtown Denver was their immediate and enthusiastic choice.

Tom studied Matt for a minute and then said:

"I'm interested in the fact that they still have the 'Light-Rail,' our old electric trolley system. And, I'm happy to hear that there still is a Colfax Avenue, which used to be Denver's main east-west thoroughfare."

"It still is Tom, however, the 'Light-Rail' is now Mag-Lev powered."

*   *   *

"May I be of any further assistance for anyone," remarked DAR as he finished removing the plates from their little dining table.

"Thank you DAR… That will be all for the time being."

DAR turned toward his wall cabinet, opened the door and stepped inside. The door closed with a subtle click and DAR was once again in 'charge' mode.

"I take it that everyone is agreeable concerning the eleven o'clock service at the National Cathedral. We should get there a little early—there may be a crowd."

"Do they know that we're coming Matt? Is this another celebrity stop?"

"That's right Tom… Might as well get used to it. Being a celebrity is not quite as much fun as most people think. However, you all can wear your newly purchased civilian clothes to this one. Remember sharp, but not, you know, the 'O' word."

"Osten—something or other," added Lilly with a smile.

"We'll all meet in the lobby at ten. How's that?"

*   *   *

At the entrance to the giant National Cathedral, which was perched boldly on the north edge of the famous Mall, a crowd had already gathered, just as Matt had warned. The people from the past still were not sure whether they were being gawked at as side-show freaks or being greeted as national heroes. The truth is that both emotions flickered across the minds of those welcoming them into their magnificent church. Even the cathedral's minister referred glowingly concerning their accomplishments, during her sermon. The service was visually beautiful and the choir's presentations were magnificent with noticeable assistance from the unparallel acoustics of the immense cathedral. However, Tom and Rob were very aware of the omissions in the liturgical portions as well as the sermon. There were no references to Heaven or Hell and there were no statements about this being, "the only *true* religion." All presentations were in English and it was an enjoyable and thrilling convocation for the young travelers and their conscientious guide.

* * *

The baseball game that afternoon was a National League affair between the Colorado Rockies and the league leading Los Angeles Dodgers. As they entered the stadium, which was located in the foothills twenty miles northwest of the city limits, Norm asked the questions that both Rob and Tom were considering:

"The Los Angeles Dodgers? I thought Los Angeles had been destroyed in the Twenty-Second Century? I thought that the LA Basin was now a bay?"

"It is Norm, but you all were probably aware that the city of Los Angeles was actually bordered to the east by the San Bernardino Mountains as well as having Mount Wilson protruding into the northeastern portion of the basin. It is here where a bold new city was built some seven hundred years ago. It is a magnificent city in the clouds. Hollywood is up there and that's where much of our great holographic entertainment originates. It is a city of two and a half million talented people and you all must visit there when you get the chance. Many great cities were finally moved to truly safer ground. New York City is still with us. It was finally rebuilt on the lands once known as Bear Mountain State Park and Harriman State Park. It is once again a thriving city of five million. Now, let's get in and see the game!"

"I hope that you have explained this to Lilly, Matt. She seemed very despondent when discussing the loss of New York when we were flying out here."

"Yes Tom—I explained it to her last night. She seemed quite relieved, however she did tell me sadly:"

"That's still not Manhattan Darling, I guess that there'll never be another Manhattan..."

During the game, the four friends discussed the similarities and differences in this modern game of baseball, when compared to the way it had been played in the earlier centuries. The consensus was that the game hadn't changed at all from when Tom, Rob and Norm were young boys. Even the athletic prowess of the players seemed essentially the same.

"What about the other sports we had in our time? What about Football, Ice Hockey; what about Basketball, Matt?"

"There still with us Norm, however, there have been some changes in sports. Some of the more brutal sports from your time have long been banned. You won't find any fighting sports anymore. Frankly, I'm surprised that these archaic sports even lasted into your time. I'm speaking of boxing and any other type of one-on-one fighting. They should have gone out with Caligula and the Roman Coliseum."

"Whoa there Matt... I was quite a fan of boxing," replied Rob.

"It was simply there, and you got interested in it when you were very young. Your elders probably told you that it was a 'manly' sport, so naturally, while growing up you emulated, or at least admired the famous fighters of your day."

"Me too Matt—I was a fan also," agreed Norm.

"Hold on... I'm not knocking you guys about this. It was natural to want to be like your big brothers or your dads. However, they still were brutal sports and eventually fell out of favor, and that happened way back in the latter part of the Twenty-First Century."

"What about the other sports Matt, what about Soccer?"

"Soccer is still with us Tom. It is probably the most popular team sport on the planet. It is simply called 'Football' to the rest of the world. Of course we already had our Football, hence the name 'Soccer.' Pardon me, I believe that you fellows were probably well aware of this little item. Anyway, we've retained most of the old sports, only the 'brutal' ones have been banned."

"Who determines which ones are the 'brutal' ones, and why do we still have our type of Football; it's pretty damned brutal? What about Ice Hockey, Matt? How brutal is that? Pardon me—I shouldn't have asked who makes the determination. I know better, of course it's the mighty UN."

"That's right Tom, it all goes back to Bern. They consider Ice Hockey and American Football as acceptable sports because they are team sports and the participants wear protective padding."

*    *    *

The baseball game, played before a packed house, ended with the home team winning five to three. As the four friends, and the now satisfied Denver fans, headed for the exit, Tom asked Matt:

"With the holographic projections so life-like at their condos, why do so many come out to the ball park? Why such good attendance?"

"Local games are 'Blacked-out' Tom."

"Of course… They did the same thing way back in our time. I think I'm getting a little slow on the up-take. Thanks for putting up with me Matt."

"Thank you guys for putting up with me. I must sound like a damned 'know-it-all,' and for this I apologize."

*    *    *

The gala evening dinner at the *new*, seven hundred year old, White House was nothing short of magnificent. There were many others, of the approximately two hundred attendees, wearing military uniforms, however, most of those had on the sparkling stars of "Flag Grade" officers. Never the less, the five new celebrities and their faithful guide, felt quite comfortable. The fact that they were seated at the head table along with President Rodriguez and his attractive wife Louise, had something to do with their ease. Joining them at the President's Table were their California Senator Gina Krieger and her husband, along with General Kincaid and his equally attractive wife. These ladies were dressed in long beautifully tailored gowns, while Senator Krieger's husband William, wore a Twentieth Century tuxedo.

As Lilly glanced around the large "State" dinning hall she noticed that all the civilian women wore formal dresses that would have been stylish in her century, and all the men's tuxedos also seemed to date back to their time. She turned back to President Rodriguez and asked about this.

"We thought it would be appropriate if we dressed in this manner for you five," came the surprising answer.

"My God… It looks like a couple of hundred people out there. They all went to the expense of purchasing formal clothing from our era, for this dinner?"

"Not just for this dinner, my Dear. Remember were going to a concert at Rachmaninov Hall afterwards."

The President smiled at Lilly and the rest of the quests in his immediate group, as he said this. At this moment, the First Lady spoke up and apologized for her husband's facetious remarks:

"His full of it Lilly… Most of our citizens have two or three formal outfits for rare occasions like this. Closets filled with formal clothes, however, would indeed be considered pretentious and not in keeping with our Democratic Socialism. David and I are allowed a few more of these garments due to the social demands of his office. And Lilly, when I say allowed, it only refers to what we all think is proper. There are no 'style police' that come around and look in one's closet to determine if they have over indulged. It is just a strong feeling that we all have to try to avoid excesses. Also, it is now considered to be correct and proper to be seen in the same dresses and jewelry at different functions and galas. Just as our gentlemen have always worn similar tuxedos for the past millennium, we ladies are expected to do so as well. Now Lilly, I must admit that I would like to keep this larger variety in clothing, that I now have as First Lady, when I return to civilian life."

Lilly smiled at this and shook her head knowingly. She then turned to her host and said:

"Well, Mister President, we are all still very flattered that all these people would go to this much trouble just for us."

"Trouble my dear… You must be joking. These people love to dress up and attend a function like this. So thank you all for helping to create this affair."

The dinner was excellent and obvious to all, the White House Chefs were real people who created real dinners from scratch. Lilly studied the individuals serving the food with a skeptical eye trying to determine if they were the fancy GAR robots or living men and women. She decided that they were human and then asked Matt. He concurred stating:

"You're beginning to get it—good girl!"

Following the splendid dinner, the guests at the head table joined the President in an escorted motorcade, that quickly covered the four blocks to Rachmaninov Hall. When they departed the hovering vehicles the crowd parted, and once again they stepped onto a long red carpet that had been rolled out for their arrival. They were led into the palatial hall and on up to their box seats by tall ushers formally dressed in stripped pants and formal tail-coats, reminiscent of a far different era.

"What about those guys Lilly? Are they, or are they not, robots?"

"They're not robots Darling. They're just handsome young men, like you dear."

"All right my fair one… I think you've got it! I *really* think you've got it! On both counts I might add."

"That's enough—*Professor Higgins*, you don't have to overdo it."

This exchange got a laugh from their buddies as well as President and Louise Rodriguez who were well aware of Rex Harrison's famous performance in "My Fair Lady."

*  *  *

The quality of the singing at the after-dinner concert was beyond any performances in Lilly's memory.

"If only Verdi and Puccini could have been alive to hear these renditions of their magnificent arias."

Lilly softly verbalized her thoughts and they were seconded by her companions.

Rob Carmody was deeply moved by the lead tenors powerful interpretation of some of the old Gallic songs of his beloved Ireland. The entire evening was a great success and everyone of the time travelers finally decided that they had now entered what seemed by all to be a better historic time for their long troubled human race.

*  *  *

That evening, after the magnificent dinner at the White House, the stunning after-dinner concert, and with all parties safely ensconced in their new quarters, Tom and Janet studied the lights of the great city from their broad twelfth floor balcony. The night air was clean and clear as it drifted up from the streets and the well maintained parks below. Tom and Janet, for the first time, focused on how pleasant each deep breath seemed. No longer were there those noxious city smells of burnt carbon based fuels rising into such balconies as the one where they now stood. A millennium of hydrogen fuel-cell powered vehicles, along with many other controls on air-pollution, had finally cleaned up the air completely.

"No wonder these 'moderns' live to be one hundred and twenty."

Tom continued searching towards the eastern horizon as he made this remark, then continued:

"Christ—, you and I might even live that long now that we are breathing air of this quality. I can feel its benefit throughout my entire body. It's an elixir sweetheart. Do you feel it as well?"

"I do darling, and I feel the same way. I feel that my entire inner body is being cleansed. God I feel good at this moment. Maybe it's having you here with me and the thought of all those future years together. It must be the air. Can you believe it—I'm high on air!"

Tom continued looking east at the bright lights that were speckled across the other buildings. He noticed that there was such a clarity, even to the more distant lights, that he could easily identify the differences in even their most subtle shades and colors.

"I also feel great Janet, and for the same reasons. Lets pray that this feeling lasts. I wonder about this compliance thing as much as you do sweetheart. But, when I look at this I'm beginning to think that it's alright. Being military people, compliance is no problem for us. It's part of the game—the ritual. We accept it," explained a now pensive Tom.

"If this new 'controlled life' has done away with poverty, and cut way back on crime, how can we not accept it?" answered Janet. "Seventy-five percent of the people on earth lived in near or actual poverty when we left Nevada. Untold millions in India and Africa existed in a life that could only be classified as a 'Living Hell.'"

"I've always felt guilty about my own status when I witnessed those TV news stories showing the starving children in Chad and Darfur. If we have to give up some of our creativity to prevent that sort of thing, then I'm willing. I guess that this really is the 'Brave New World,' Janet."

Tom said this with a rather dramatic sweep of his right hand indicating the breadth and majesty of their new capital city, Denver, Colorado. He studied Janet's delicate face, which was now framed by those colorful sparkling lights of the other plush forty story tall condominiums stretching across the eastern portion of Denver, which was still known by its name of his youth, Aurora. Somehow that name fit the area more than ever. Janet had never appeared more beautiful to him as she closely studied the benevolent expression of her man. She then sat down on the small balcony bench and motioned for him to sit beside her. Following this, she once again looked out towards the city lights and responded slowly and with emotion:

"Alright now Tom… I discussed this next subject with Lilly, and she agrees."

"I know—and also agree. Matt brought it up during our little 'pit stop' at the concert and it seems that we are all in agreement. The reason I know what this 'next subject' is about, is because I've also noticed that you call me Tom when it's something serious. I'm totally with you on this one Janet—it is serious."

"Okay honey… You obviously know, or I should say *knew* this town very well. Where do you want the services to be held? After all it's going to be a double wedding. We won't need a large facility because I can only think of two guests. I don't believe we'll need any wedding invitations either."

Tom leaned forward and studied the bright marigolds that lined the wooden planter in front of the polished railing.

"I think Matt's already working on this one Sweetheart. I believe that all the large churches are downtown and all of them are new to me. I doubt that there are any of the churches of my youth still standing."

"We're letting Matt handle this? I'm not so sure about this Tom. Matt and Lilly don't seemed to be committed to any religion."

"From the way these briefings have gone, I don't believe anyone now is *committed* to any particular religion."

"We'll Tom, your still Episcopalian and I'm still Lutheran. I would still like to have a religious or at least a church wedding ceremony."

Tom stood up, turned and faced his beautiful fiancé. He spoke slowly and with a hint of emotion:

"Matt also confided something else to me, however, he wanted to be the one to tell you. I think, after you hear this, that you might be alright with him handling the plans for the wedding ceremony. He has spoken privately with Senator Krieger a number of times during the past two days. He learned that there is a beautiful little chapel in the White House."

"You're kidding... The White House again! Wow! Okay Sweetheart—I'm really in. I definitely approve!"

"Hold on honey... I didn't say that this had been approved by the President. However Gina Krieger told Matt that Louise Rodriguez likes the idea. It seems that Gina and the First Lady are rather close friends."

"Close friends... That's it! We're going to get married in the White House. Wow!"

"Just one more thing honey, Gina intimated that there will be a few more than two guests attending. How about two hundred?"

"Wow!"

Janet came to her feet and joined her beloved at the railing. She put her arms around him and drew him into a sensuous kiss.

"Maybe this was the right time after all, to tell you about this."

"I think so Darling—I really think so."

The two happy young lovers then stared out once again at the vast expanse of their capitol city that stretched across the eastern horizon. They stood there silently for some time before Janet broke the spell and voiced some lingering worries that she still harbored concerning their future and this new environment.

"Implant or not my darling, I'm still not totally satisfied with the status-quo. I think we can do better! 'Life Leases?' No true ownership of real property? Reprogramming? Franchises? Euthanasia! Spring is Fall! Socialism! Pardon me Tom—I guess it's just my nature to bitch!"

"Don't apologize sweetheart. There's an old saying from the past that goes something like this:

'If women didn't bitch, *all* of us would still be naked, dirty, sleeping in caves and throwing rocks at each other!'"

"Very funny Dear, and please don't forget it... Seriously Tom, this seems to be a better world. Maybe we human occupants have actually turned the corner. Truly, I now believe that this really is a better world even with implant assisted compliance, and for once in our convoluted and pain filled history, we the 'enlightened species' do *not* seem to be headed for self-destruction!"

Janet turned back towards the partially open sliding glass door to their balcony. She hadn't heard anything unusual, yet she sensed a presence and she was a little startled to see DAR standing in the doorway. The robot was barely visible in the pale evening light, but its green eyes seemed to have taken on an unusual intensity as it stepped rather boldly out onto the balcony. At this moment, Tom turned from the railing and both astronauts faced their Domestic Assistance Robot.

In a precise mechanical voice DAR rather succinctly announced:

"It's time for both of you to come inside—right now… I'll lock the slider behind you."

Although the young couple wanted to prolong these pleasurable moments at the railing while staring out at the colorful lights of the great city; they both felt a new and rather disturbing emotion. Both of them now felt compelled to *submit* to the little robot's softly spoken request. The two lovers entered the apartment, then DAR locked the sliding glass door after following them inside. Janet clearly heard, and even felt, the sharp metallic click of the slider's lock, and now she really began to wonder:

*What's really going on in this "better world" of the Fourth Millennium…?*

Certainly not THE END

## SKY PAINTER

**To dreamers and explorers…**

*A magnificent sky stretched before me above*
*Clouds drifting here and there lost in search*
*Dreams with fables of grand tales heroes made*
*As I lay by my paints and brushes in this glade…*

*Still higher my mind wanders drawn to colors*
*Soaring in majestic circles with many others*
*Parting my spirit leaps from my body to fly*
*In peace with harmony towards this distant sky…*

*Breaking free now of earth's persistent hold*
*I venture with my journey past my sun of gold*
*The darkened black of midnight calls out night*
*As I continue upwards and out in visions flight…*

*Mars, then Venus in silent movement below I see*
*Beacons of life long ago, far from you and me*
*Leaving this lonely star system farther behind*
*Only here I travel in my still dreaming mind…*

*Stars surround me in shades of galactic blends*
*Telling stories of light closer than any lens*
*To paint these many galaxies of swirling bright*
*I look to my palate of red, yellow and white…*

*Finally to those who will search the stars above*
*Carry my words aloft and now conceived in love*
*Adrift on heaven's ocean on this speck of sand*
*Live dreamers, poets and sky painters called man.*

**Stephen W. Round**
"Poets, painters and writers will explore space as our future unfolds."